Beyond the window, he saw shapes moving through the gardens. He squinted at them, but quickly realized that it was not gardeners at work.

Three figures...no, four. A woman with a babe on her hip and two small boys were running away from the manor.

Laura was leaving—again—and taking his children this time!

Panicked, he flung the window wide and jumped out in pursuit.

He caught up with them on the maze path. "Where the hell do you think you're going?"

"I thought it obvious."

"Take them back inside," he ordered.

Laura's chin rose. "No."

Nash caught her arm. "You dare defy me?"

"Oh, I dare." Her gaze slowly lifted to his. "I'm no meek lamb to the slaughter anymore."

Surrender Becomes Her

Heather Boyd

CHAPTER ONE

RAVENSWOOD PALACE WAS every bit as grand and imposing as Lady Laura Sweet remembered, but for all its opulence it was an utterly horrible place to live. Laura felt unwell as she drew closer. Yet she did not resist as her brother-in-law, Jasper, drew her on to take tea in the duke's drawing room for a discussion long overdue.

Laura glanced down at her infant daughter in her arms, Isabelle, seeking reassurance in her tiny face that she'd made the right decision to come back now. She had already abandoned her sons to her husband and his family, and now she would be required to do so with Isabelle. But there hadn't been a day when she'd not longed for her sons.

They had grown so much while she was away. Skipping innocently through

Ravenswood's hallowed halls ahead of her now. Liam did not remember her. Thomas might, not that he wanted to show it.

She knew what to expect. Shouting and a cold shoulder. Banishment in the end. Banishment she could live with. Being forced to stay and treated for her alleged illness she would not endure again.

Laura paused in the doorway of the drawing room and shivered as she heard footsteps following behind. "Nothing ever changes here."

"It will be all right," Jasper promised, giving her arm a brief squeeze.

No, it would not be. Her days here had been fraught with loneliness and despair. The old duke grew to dislike her and had not bothered to hide that fact. But he'd liked her dowry and pressed Nash to use it to fund his lavish excesses, while Nash scrimped on her and made her a virtual prisoner here.

Nash had been too preoccupied by the old duke's business to provide any protection. He had never stood up to his father, and they had argued about how their children were being raised in near seclusion on the estate. She'd tried to convince Nash to take her and the children away from Ravenswood once, but he had refused to abandon his brothers and put his own family first.

She took a seat beside the fire and did not look around to see if her husband's shuttered expression had changed at all from when she'd arrived.

The duke swept past her to stand at the mantelpiece. "Sister. It seems like only yesterday since you sat in that exact spot, brightening the room," the Duke of Ravenswood murmured.

"I'm surprised anyone noticed I was gone," she replied without bothering to hide her sarcasm. Only the physician the last duke paid to bleed her just so she could visit her children would have felt the loss—to his pocketbook—when she'd fled.

"We *all* felt your absence most keenly." A softer smile appeared on the duke's face as he regarded Isabelle again. "And as for this little one, Mama would have been pleased to know her family tradition continued, too. First-born daughters on her side were often called Isabelle."

Laura frowned at him, confused by his buoyant mood. "I expected you would disapprove of my taking the honor from your children, Your Grace."

"I'm sure you did, and I'm glad I could surprise you." Ravenswood shrugged carelessly. "I dislike the habit of repeating given names, to be honest. It causes confusion. I hope my wife will concoct something original."

Laura glanced around, expecting to see a duchess at any moment, but she, whoever she was, did not appear. "Congratulations, Your Grace," she murmured.

"For what?"

"For making a marriage," she said. "Jasper did not tell me the happy news."

Ravenswood laughed heartily. "My dear sister, you are far too early to offer any congratulations." His gaze turned aside, his eyes narrowed on Jasper and Mrs. Radcliffe, who sat close together. "I had set myself the task of marrying off my brothers first."

"You did not," Jasper protested. "It was only you we talked about getting leg-shackled."

The duke nodded, and his gaze flickered toward the doorway. "And yet you all are married, or soon will be. We will discuss the date of your future nuptials in short order, Jasper. Nash?"

Jasper stood up. "*If* Sophie wants to be married quickly, then she shall decide when and where, and it will not be up to you or Nash."

Ravenswood scowled at his younger brother, who was now standing with his arms about his future bride. "Where is Nash?"

"How should I know? I'm not his keeper."

Laura shook her head. So, Nash had not bothered to join them. He must be truly vexed that she'd dared return. Well, he was going to be further stunned when he heard what she had come here to tell him.

She'd come back only to make their separation permanent.

Isabelle touched her face, and she smiled down at her beautiful child. The secret she'd kept from him. So precious, so trusting, so unaware yet that a father might never show her an ounce of affection.

She met the duke's gaze. "I should express my condolences for the loss of your parent," she murmured, wishing her late father-in-law a merry time in hell.

The duke wagged his finger at her, "Now, now, my dear sister. Don't spoil our reunion by mouthing condolences you couldn't possibly mean. We all know my father liked none of us, especially you."

She narrowed her gaze at the duke. The late duke had been a nasty man, but she had not thought Ravenswood would admit to that out loud. "As you say."

"I do say." Ravenswood leaned an elbow upon the mantelpiece and studied her, clearly amused by that. "Our father wouldn't enjoy this moment of family reunion at all, but he no longer matters. We are all free of his interference at last."

She raised a brow at his remark. "And instead, we must endure yours?"

Jasper laughed, and Sophie silenced him.

"Touché, my dear." Ravenswood's grin widened. "Indeed, yes. What an excellent idea, my lady. We shall do things my way from now on. Mrs. Radcliffe, might we impose on your excellent governess skills one last time to take the children away for a little while? I will be forever in your debt. Jasper can go with you if that is any consolation."

"No," Nash barked, making the children all jump at the harsh sound.

Laura had startled as well, and she had to soothe her daughter, too. She glanced around to discover Nash standing not far away, feet planted wide, arms folded across his chest, scowling at everyone in the room.

Ravenswood peeled himself away from the mantelpiece. "He speaks?"

"Barely a sentence, though," Laura couldn't help but mutter to herself.

It was Sophie who laughed this time.

"I'm not letting her out of my sight again," Nash announced so forcefully that Laura shivered again and hugged Isabelle a little tighter against her.

"Then, by all means, take a seat," Ravenswood ordered. "You're looking a little flushed, brother, from the warmth of the day...or is it the beauty of your wife's face that affects you still?"

Laura scoffed. "I assure you that any warmth he's feeling toward me is solely in your imagination, Your Grace."

"I wouldn't be so sure," Ravenswood warned but turned away to lean against the mantelpiece again, eyes flickering back and forth between them.

Nash resumed his stance of stoic silence and would not meet her gaze. He would not welcome her home or forbid her return either, it seemed. He would let the Duke of Ravenswood do all his talking still.

Laura waited patiently for the duke's interrogation to continue.

Thomas and Liam edged closer, and she patted the cushion beside her, hoping they would sit down. They should have been taken away but she was glad for any time she got to spend with them now. The late duke always forced them to stand in his presence. But with one throat clearing from their father, their backs straightened as if they dared not move a muscle.

Even though she expected it, it hurt a great deal to see them so stiff and obedient. She'd had no control over their lives and no choice but to leave them behind. She hadn't even been allowed to see them without a servant being present by the end.

"Nash, sit."

Of course, her husband obeyed the duke's order.

Ravenswood sat down next to his brother too, but Nash jiggled his knee as if he couldn't stand being in the same room with her.

Jasper moved into the spot by her side and gave her a reassuring smile. When Laura looked around for the governess, she discovered the woman had slipped away.

She faced the duke, knowing Nash would never start this conversation. "You wished to speak with me?"

The duke sat forward, eyes bright with interest, folding his hands between his knees. "For years."

They stared at each other a few moments more, but the duke then glanced sideways at Nash. He grimaced. "Jasper, vacate that seat for our brother to sit upon instead."

Jasper jumped up, but Nash did not move so much as a muscle.

The duke rolled his eyes, "Do it! Sit over there beside your wife so I might see you together again."

Reluctantly, her husband moved. Laura didn't watch him, but she felt him draw close. His passage produced no breeze, but she shivered anyway as he sat as far away from her as possible on the settee.

"Now, that is somewhat better. Let us begin."

"It's obvious I cannot be married to this woman," Nash announced bluntly.

"I no longer wish to be married to this man either," Laura added, making sure her voice was heard loud and clear by everyone in the room. "That is the only reason I have returned."

They were not good for each other. Separation had been lonely but a relief. She'd found a measure of peace in her temporary home.

"Well, at least you agree on something," the duke exclaimed. "However, I am not convinced a separation is the right course of action at this time."

Nash sat forward and glared at the duke. "It is not your decision to make."

"There's no doubt in my mind the marriage was a mistake," Laura added. "I could not endure it again."

"Were Thomas, Liam and now Isabelle a mistake?"

She glanced at her sons and saw confusion in their eyes. They edged closer to Nash. "No, they are not a mistake. I love *all* of my children."

"*My* sons should leave us now," Nash announced.

"No, you wanted the children to stay so they stay," Ravenswood commanded. "All of them belong here. Everything about this discussion will affect them and their future."

"I disagree," Nash argued. "I am the boys' father, and the decision is solely mine to decide what they are privy to hearing."

"Then be their father," Jasper threw out. "An annulment would make them the children of no one."

"I did not intend for that to happen. The boys will remain my legitimate heirs. I will petition for a divorce. There are clear grounds for a claim of adultery."

Laura sucked in a sharp breath. Nash was wrong. She'd never so much as looked at another man besides him.

The duke studied her, and his eyes dropped to Isabelle. The corners of his mouth lifted into a grin after a moment. "Isabelle is most definitely your daughter because you are still married to each other, brother. And the record of her birth clearly states you are her father."

Laura gasped in shock that he'd known about Isabelle, which meant Nash had also known about their little girl.

The duke winked at her. "I have my sources."

Laura closed her eyes, irritated by the loose lips of someone she'd trusted, but oddly grateful for it as well. Isabelle must be recognized as Nash's legitimate offspring if their daughter was to have the future she deserved. A place in society and a dowry for when she was old enough to be wed.

Nash sat forward again, glaring at the duke. "You knew she had a child and didn't tell me?"

"If you'd gone after her like I kept suggesting you should, you would have discovered it for yourself," Ravenswood argued back. "Your shock today is your own damn fault."

Nash burst out of his chair.

"Don't you dare walk away from this," Ravenswood barked, standing up as well. "Isabelle is a fact, and your daughter. There will be no divorce citing adultery unless it is *yours*."

Laura held her breath and let the brothers battle wills across the room. It was no surprise that Nash relented and sat down again. He always did what Algernon asked him to do.

Even propose to Laura in his place, she suspected now.

"There was no adultery. You clearly shared her bed after she left the estate, and this is the result, isn't it?" Algernon asked, a question in his eyes when he glanced her way.

Laura inclined her head to confirm but did not share the details of when it had happened to avoid her own embarrassment.

She'd not informed Nash about the pregnancy, fearing his father would take the child away from her or drag her back to Ravenswood for the birth and the *cure* for the melancholy that came after.

Ravenswood narrowed his eyes. "Nash? Do you acknowledge your obligation? Isabelle's reputation must remain above reproach if she is to have any sort of future in our society and our family."

Laura stared at the duke in astonishment. She had not expected him to be her ally in this matter at all.

After a moment, her husband growled out a "yes".

Laura breathed a sigh of relief. Nash had taken responsibility for their child and her future was secure. That was all Laura wanted, besides her own freedom.

"Good. Now that the matter is settled, Jasper can take all the children away now to find his betrothed," the duke asked. Nash did not protest this time.

Jasper drew closer. "Stand firm, sister. I'm on your side forever, remember? I'll see you at dinner."

Laura hoped to be long gone by then, but she appreciated Jasper's offer of support. It could not be easy to be the only one in the family who thought well of her. She kissed Isabelle and handed her daughter to him. "Goodbye, Jasper. Take care of her."

"I would, but she has you," he said, smiling.

Laura lowered her eyes as Jasper lured her sons from the room with him and Isabelle, promising the boys a treat from the kitchen after they found Mrs. Radcliffe.

She fought back tears but steadied herself. "I've shared the bed of no other man and nor have I ever wanted to."

"It is a relief to hear that. Isn't it, Nash?" the duke murmured. "Fidelity in a marriage is so very important."

Laura glanced at Nash just as he looked at her, his face turning an unbecoming shade of red. Was he embarrassed they'd slept together again after she'd left him? Or did he not even remember their night together?

He had been very much in his cups, and it might be possible for him to have no memory.

She straightened her spine. "If there's nothing else, I would like to discuss the divorce and then speak to my children before I go."

"Unlike last time," Nash muttered.

"Actually, there is no need for you to leave," Ravenswood suggested. "Every effort will be made to make your homecoming as smooth as possible."

"There's no point her staying. We don't wish to be married to each other, so she might as well leave immediately," Nash cut in.

Laura expected Nash's attitude but eyed the duke with deep suspicion because he opposed Nash's wishes. "I am happy to go."

"Don't be too hasty." The duke held up both hands. "Divorce is a complicated business. Without the use of a claim of adultery, it will be difficult for Nash to make a strong case. We will discuss the matter over the next month."

Nash burst to his feet again. "I'll not wait that long."

Laura shook her head. "Nor will I."

"The poor state of your relations is not my only concern. I have other business to attend to and Jasper's marriage to plan for now, as well. As head of the family, I need time to become familiar with the legalities and requirements of a petition for divorce, and your marriage contract, too, I might add."

Laura sighed. She had suspected it would not be easy. The terms of her marriage to Nash had been thrashed out by their fathers behind closed doors. Even so, she'd known they had argued heatedly over the terms, but Father had prevailed with as much protection and pin money for her as possible.

"She can wait for news wherever she used to

live," Nash suggested, throwing up his hands and turning away.

"Well, that is too far away for me," Ravenswood argued. "I have many questions, and you two," he picked up a large hourglass, "will both spend the turning of *this* in conversation with each other in front of me answering them."

Nash sputtered.

Laura choked. "What questions could you possibly have for us? Don't you know everything about everyone?"

"I am not my father. And I wish to avoid a similar fate to your situation when I take a bride. I wish to learn from your mistakes and study the terms of your marriage contract in detail."

But Laura could not believe that. She suspected the duke was trying to manipulate a reconciliation between them just to avoid a scandal and paying her portion. Was *that* why Ravenswood suggested this delay? Out of fear Nash might have to return a hefty portion of her dowry?

Laura shook her head, unwilling to yield to such terms for no benefit. "What good will come of an hour spent together when he will not speak and hardly looks at me?"

The duke smiled. "You will be supervised during your conversations. Deliberate silence beyond one minute will not be tolerated."

"I'll not be bullied by you or punished for disobedience," Laura warned him, standing up. "I had enough of that from your late father."

"The threat isn't meant for you, dear," Ravenswood answered, his attention firmly on Laura's husband. "It's him. The situation here, within the family, has changed markedly since my father's demise. But make no mistake, I am in control now. If you don't want to cooperate, I have ways and means of making you vastly uncomfortable. I know all the secrets you'd prefer not be shared, Nash."

Laura raised a brow, intrigued by a threat aimed not at her, but at her husband for once.

Perhaps the brothers were not as close as they once were, but it made no difference to her situation. Isabelle had been acknowledged as Nash's legitimate offspring and she would eventually have her freedom.

She would suffer any temporary discomfort to be spared continuing a marriage with Nash. If that meant she had to spend one last month being ignored, so be it. She'd have more time to spend with her sons and she could work on Ravenswood to speed up proceedings, perhaps even convince him to allow her additional visitation rights after the divorce was final.

It could be to her benefit to agree with the duke's request for now.

"Very well. I will give you thirty days more of my life and my complete cooperation in pursuit of a divorce, provided I can be with my children without supervision."

"I won't stop you, but perhaps you won't want a divorce in the end," Ravenswood answered, eyes still on Nash.

She nodded. "I'm sure I still will."

"Nash, escort your wife upstairs to the nursery. From today, you will be taking over the many duties of your last governess together."

"I had another servant in training for that position already," Nash ground out.

"Oh, no. I'll not waste wages on another governess when there's so much work to go round already. The two of you will care for your three children alone from the moment they wake till they are put to bed each night, with only help from the cook and one maid at night to sleep with them. The Ravenswood servants will not come to your rescue."

Laura hid a smile. When she'd lived here before, she had not been allowed to have any say over her children's daily routine. The old duke had left her out of all important discussions, and so had Nash. To suddenly be given total responsibility for them for thirty days was a gift she would treasure for the rest of her life. No doubt Nash would never stir himself to become more involved with them, which meant she'd hardly ever see him outside their hourglass conversation each day.

"I've no objection," she said.

"Good." The duke waved her away. "That will be all for now."

Laura turned for the door.

"Laura, please wait for your husband to escort you up the stairs," Ravenswood called out.

"I'm done waiting for him," she answered.

CHAPTER TWO

"YOU'VE no idea what you've done," Nash ground out the minute Laura left the room.

Algernon laughed heartily.

"This isn't funny," Nash growled.

Algernon wiped at his eyes. "Come now, brother. This is best for all of us, especially the children, and Jasper."

"What has Jasper to do with you giving my wife carte blanch? She can't be trusted to stay," he promised, utterly furious with her for coming back now—and looking so damn appealing.

"Sophie would never abandon those children without knowing someone was looking after them," Algernon warned.

"Like my wife did so easily," he ground out.

"Come now. I doubt it was easy for her at all. Laura left them with her nursemaid and us, and you could have stopped her going if you'd tried," Algernon claimed.

Nash shook his head. "How could I have stopped her when she waited until we were all gone from the estate to leave?"

"Well, if Father had been here, she'd have never escaped," Algernon warned. "You could have gone after her."

"What good would that have done?" he asked but turned away, stomach still in knots from his first sighting of his runaway wife.

Laura looked remarkably unchanged, but defiant, despite the years he'd been sunk in misery after she'd departed.

Algernon was silent for a few long moments. "Tell me you didn't want her to go."

No, he hadn't wanted that. Not really. Nash turned back slowly to face his brother. "Father was difficult about her."

Algernon crossed the room to thump him on the shoulder. "You blithering idiot. You *did* want her to leave? Why didn't you tell me?"

"I did not want her to leave me, or the children the way she did." He sighed and dropped into a chair near the fire, the one Laura had just vacated. "What I wished for then was for Father to keep his nose out of my business with my wife."

"Well, this is a damn mess we can't avoid dealing with anymore," Algernon warned.

"Honestly, it is not all bad. Now that I know my feelings about the marriage are reciprocated, I will continue with my pursuit of a divorce with or without your support. I accepted the responsibility of Laura's daughter, so she will not fight me on the issue. She obviously hates me."

"A divorce will only make things ten times worse. Think of the scandal. Think of the money that must be given back."

"She'll get the money owed to her somehow, and she'll be happier," Nash promised, tilting his head back to look at the plastered ceiling instead of facing his brother's gaze.

He'd never made Laura happy and probably never could. It had taken today's events, losing a governess to his brother and learning he'd been cuckolded, to make him understand he did not inspire loyalty from women.

"And what about the children? They need their mother."

"I never thought she'd stay away from them for so long. I imagined she'd at least try to see them, but..."

"But she didn't. She had no friends left in the district once Father had finished maligning her character. No one would have dared help her."

"Yes," he said uneasily. Laura had not come

home, even for the funerals of her last relatives. She'd hidden herself far away from all of them. Despite Algernon's suggestion, he had tried to find her for a time, but without success.

"Well, some part of her family home must still be livable because I rightly guessed that she had been camped out in the ruins. There was mud on her boots. We must look into that."

Nash was curious about that, too. The adjoining estate where Laura had grown up had fallen to further ruin after the fire that had destroyed it. Her late brother's will had not been found, so the matter of who would inherit the estate, and repair it, remained uncertain. "*I* will look into it. He was my brother-in-law."

"Jasper might stand a better chance of finding out something from her about a likely location of her brother's last will and testament. They were close once upon a time," Algernon suggested with a smirk. "He's also had more to do with her while we were gone than he revealed, too."

"Yes, that seems obvious to me as well," Nash agreed, grinding his teeth over that betrayal. Being the last to know his wife had borne someone, a stranger, a daughter, burned. "Despite her claim otherwise, Laura forsook her marriage vows. Perhaps Jasper can find out who I can name in the divorce."

Algernon settled opposite him. "Are you sure the child could not be yours?"

He shook his head, bitterness welling. "I never saw Laura again after she left the estate. The child cannot be mine."

"But doesn't she look so much like the other pair at that age?"

"Yes, there is a similarity." But then he shook his head firmly. "The child was born when? Last winter? So conception must have taken place the spring before that. I did not see Laura last year at all. I was in London for the season with you." He gulped. "We had not been intimate since she left me the year before that."

There'd only been one occasion in that time when he'd shared a bed, a settee really, with a woman, and Algernon did not need to know about that indiscretion. Nash himself had broken his vows, the very night he'd first considered the pursuit of a divorce.

A beguiling woman had singled him out at a London masquerade at the end of the season, and amid the darkness and indulgence of too much wine, he had succumbed to his loneliness with her. It was a night that he was still ashamed of, and he'd been so drunk he could barely remember much of the event, or her, besides the uncontrollable need to kiss her.

He hadn't been looking for company or a

woman to please. But that night, he had been swept away and satisfied in a manner he hadn't been for a long time. Not since Laura, in fact. The woman disappeared before the unmasking, so he'd never found out who she might have been.

"So you've made love to no one since Laura then?"

"Yes," Nash lied.

But around the time he'd been in bed with a stranger in London, Laura must have been cuckolding him with some other man somewhere else. A man who'd no doubt felt as lucky as *he'd* always felt when Laura had turned to him in the dark and welcomed him with open arms.

The way his lover had done that night in London.

He shut his eyes, remembering that night with sharper clarity—and then opened them wide in shock. *"Devil take it!"*

His lover had been determined to keep her mask on at all times and told him to close his eyes...and today Laura had sworn the child was his.

Could the lady who seduced him last year have been Laura?

He raked a hand through his hair, astonished he might not have recognized his wife in the dark.

Algernon drew closer, smirking. "I gather you recall a forgotten rendezvous?"

He sat down, shocked. "My wife seduced me."

"I imagine she enjoyed that," Algernon murmured, failing to hide the merriment in his tone.

Nash ground his teeth and snarled, "Oh, she did. She was satisfied beyond the shadow of a doubt, even as drunk as I must have been."

Laura had made a fool out of him! She'd kept him enthralled beneath her the whole time they'd made love. He also recalled being denied his release, even when he pleaded for it, and there had been such desperation in the end that his control had suffered.

The guilt he'd carried over that indiscretion was slow to ease from his chest. It had been a night of pure, unadulterated wickedness that never would have happened had he had his wits about him.

But the next moment, he thought of all he'd missed because of that one careless, decadent night, and his anger returned full force. "That witch," he growled.

"Nash, you cannot be angry with a wife who could not keep her hands out of your trousers," Algernon whispered. "Drunk or not, it took your willing participation to make that child. Congratulations. It will be quite the novelty, having a niece to play with."

"A daughter I never planned for," Nash added.

Yes, he was as much to blame for Isabelle's existence as Laura. He had unbuttoned his own trousers. He would never forgive himself for that. "I would have wanted to know about the pregnancy. To be present for the birth, as I had been for our sons. I would have wanted to have been first to hold my daughter."

"Given your new clarity and admissions, there is no further debate needed," Algernon said. "I will record Isabelle's name in the family bible, and Laura *will* be afforded all the rights and privileges as a member of this family as she always should have been. That includes pin money and unrestricted access to her children at all times," the duke announced. "You cannot play the tyrant."

"When have I ever?"

"Or play the victim to me instead. You know what you are like. Stomping and glaring when you don't like what you hear. You always have trouble letting go. You like things neat and on a schedule. Laura has always been more impulsive than you. You will have to start again with her and share the burden of your decisions."

"So we can divorce?"

"So you can exist with peace in your hearts. A divorce might solve one problem between you, but you will continue to be the parents of three impressionable children. It would not do for them to see you both constantly bickering. You remember how Mother and Father were? I do not wish that childhood on anyone."

Nash's heart hurt as he thought of his youth. The anxiety and constant fear of failing to meet high expectations. Trying to please two demanding parents who were constantly at war—even after Mother died.

History had already repeated itself with him and Laura. His impossible wife. In arm's reach for only a short time and still so far beyond him. She hadn't changed. She possessed the same curves that had always appealed to him, even when he could not see her face, apparently. Same unruly brown hair, always ready to escape its confinement. He had loved to toy with her locks as she slept after the rush of lovemaking was over. To feel the tension leave them both at the end of a long and trying day.

Her eyes were the same dark shade of brown, but flinty and distrustful when she regarded him now.

She used to smile more.

He met his older brother's gaze and shook his head. "You're wrong to keep her here."

"Thirty days is not a lifetime sentence." The smile fell from Algernon's face. "Would you rather I drive her away immediately instead? To be as cruel as Father and keep you so out of things so that we never know what was going on here? That would solve everything for you, wouldn't it, if she'd have just slunk away or even died?"

Nash's eyes widened. "I never said I want her dead."

"If looks could kill, she'd be done for today. I did not think it possible for you to act as cold and unfeeling as Father was, but damn it, brother, it is a day of celebration and damned if I will be as miserable as you." Algernon shook his head. "Who could imagine Jasper and your governess would fall in love? She's perfect for him, though. And Laura coming back is perfectly timed, since they seem to want to run off together. My heart is infinitely lighter for seeing Laura again. How can you not feel more?"

"I don't know what I feel," he admitted, unaccustomed to revealing so much. Laura was a subject that only led to an argument between them.

"No matter what I said today in front of Laura, I will not support this divorce. The resulting scandal would destroy us."

"You mean destroy *you*," Nash murmured.

"Me, us, what difference does it make?" Algernon said. "We are a family. Our successes and failures reflect on each other. People whisper about the sorry state of your marriage already and a divorce will ensure the gossips' tongues will never lie still. Think of how the women of the family will fare, too. Win, Amity, Sophie and our other female cousins. Instead of having the favor of society, they will be drawn into a scandal with you and Laura. Laura will be the only one spared, because if you divorce her, I can almost guarantee she will disdain society."

Nash nodded, agreeing with him.

"And you, the man I have depended on my entire life, will become a pariah. Wanted nowhere when I need you most of all. Any match I might want to make will be indelibly tainted by talk of your divorce. I cannot imagine Lady Stephanie Kent wanting anything to do with me, should you go through with your plan. And as you have so often pointed out, we need her money rather desperately."

Nash ground his teeth, annoyed that he agreed with all of his brother's assessments of what a divorce might do to their standing in society and attempts to fix their financial woes. The latter was why Nash had chosen Sophie to be his next bride.

Sophie would have inherited some funds one day, and he'd thought she would not want to take part in the London season to be whispered about. But it seems he never really knew Sophie, either.

Her heart had been claimed by Jasper while Nash's back was turned.

"Perhaps you should have wed Lady Stephanie when you had the chance."

Algernon threw his arms wide. "How was I to know what you intended? I'm not a mind reader. Nor is your wife, thank God."

"What is that supposed to mean?"

"Hadn't you just finished telling us you wished to marry Sophie? Seeing your wife standing side by side with the woman meant to replace her can only be described as bloody awkward for me."

Nash winced. For himself, as well. He'd been rather stunned and had not known what to say to Jasper. "I was unaware of Jasper's interest in Sophie when I unwisely spoke of my plans earlier. Did you know about them?"

"No, but it makes sense she would be the one to turn his head. He's always liked a challenge, and he found fault with the governess almost since the day she arrived. Your talk of marrying her upset him when we returned, and at the time, I thought it was only on Laura's behalf."

"Yes, he was unusually opinionated today," Nash mused. In fact, Jasper had never once spoken his mind so clearly before. He had changed while Nash hadn't been paying attention.

"Jasper has made his choice. You'll have to accept the match graciously, though it's obviously not what you hoped for."

Nash nodded. He had to let the idea of a second marriage go for now, too, most likely. He should wait until Algernon was finally wed before proceeding. Nothing was turning out the way he'd expected.

"Take a moment to get your bearings. It's clear to see that Laura's return has upset you, so get over that as soon as you can," Algernon suggested. "Emotions are running high all over today. Gads, we both need a drink."

Nash refused a glass and looked down at his clenched hands. He needed to keep his wits about him.

Algernon had always been far more agile than him when it came to the unexpected. Gentle when he needed to be, a battering ram when required. Nash needed to focus on what he could do, not what he wanted to do. Laura would be at Ravenswood for only one month. He could try to make peace with her, for the sake of their children.

Algernon moved away, leaving Nash staring at his fists. He uncurled his hands slowly. Some time ago, he had removed his wedding band out of necessity. But the mark, the depression, was still there on his finger, and he rubbed at it now, as he often did when he thought of his wife.

He had not handled the moment of seeing her again very well, but he'd never been at his ease around his bride. Not outside the bedchamber, anyway. In bed, he knew exactly how to behave.

Seeing her again had been a great shock.

But he should make an effort to be civil while Laura remained under the same roof as him. But if she was to resume her adjoining bedchamber, he would have to prevent any further attempts at seduction on her part. That was a threshold they should never cross again.

Three children were more than enough for a marriage that was in tatters.

His marriage to Laura had been awkward from the start. Sudden matches often were. Laura, at seventeen, had been beautiful and accomplished, but their father had wished for her to become Algernon's bride and the future Duchess of Ravenswood, rather than Nash's.

Everyone had expected that match—until the last moment.

When Algernon had suddenly vowed he'd never marry, just to spite their father, Laura had quickly agreed to a marriage to Nash, the spare, to avoid any embarrassment and damage to her reputation.

He closed his eyes, remembering the terror of the moment when he'd proposed in Algernon's place. It had been a stormy night and that should have been an omen for how they would live as man and wife. He'd been so nervous about getting the unexpected words out right, but Laura hadn't seemed to notice his clumsiness. She'd agreed with a soft sigh he'd mistaken for contentment.

Unfortunately, their married life had failed to meet her high expectations in almost every respect bar one. He had given her the children she'd said she longed for. Only to have another by him in secret. "How long have you known about the girl?"

"I didn't."

Nash pursed his lips. "Why did you lie about knowing, then?"

"I was attempting to delay a discussion about her adultery until you'd recovered your composure. However, clearly she did nothing wrong, nor did you."

Nash could feel his face heating. "So you really believe she is mine?"

"Isabelle looks much like the other pair did at that age," Algernon mused. "I can't imagine another man would have shared Laura's bed. She never seemed the type for half measures. Father was quite wrong to blacken her character the way he so often tried to do."

"Father distrusted all women," Nash murmured.

"I was always grateful we never had sisters after I saw how he behaved toward Laura," Algernon said. "But now he's gone and we're overrun with females."

Nash hunched a little at the observation.

It shouldn't matter that theirs was not an expected match, but it always did to him. The marriage had served its purpose. Father's purpose was all that had mattered once. What remained of Laura's dowry had gone to the dukedom now, though. He would be repaid one day. His oldest son would inherit, should Algernon fail to marry and produce legitimate heirs. Thomas and Liam had always been the duchy's insurance against such a thing.

Laura had not agreed with him about that... not that she'd ever agreed with him about anything after Liam had arrived.

He turned as he heard a thump to find Algernon had left the drawing room and was halfway up a ladder in the library, stripping book after book from the floor-to-ceiling bookshelves and talking to himself.

"Where the hell is it?"

He hurried across the hall to offer his help. "What are you looking for?"

"The legal books Father used to keep behind his desk to hit us with. I had them all put up here when I took over."

"They have been in my book room since the day after the funeral."

Algernon slid down the ladder and turned to glare at Nash. "You were planning the divorce even before we left for the summer house party?"

"Of course I was," he admitted. "This is not a rushed decision, but a long-considered one."

"Well, go fetch those and any other volumes you've appropriated. I'll be much too busy in the coming weeks to chase all over the house after them all." When Nash did not move, Algernon barked, "Go!"

Stung by the manner of his dismissal, a reminder of how Father had talked to him, Nash stalked off toward the other side of the palace. He was grateful, though, to have a chore that did not require him to think beyond the immediate future because his mind was in a whirl and might never settle again.

CHAPTER THREE

LAURA LET herself into the nursery and leaned against the heavy door, panting from her rush to escape the icy stare and company of her now visibly angry husband.

She'd thought she was ready for that, but apparently she was not immune to his moods. He believed she had betrayed him. He was wrong. Things would have been easier and so much simpler if she had shared a bed with someone else.

She let out a shaky breath and then quickly glanced around the large nursery room. Her sons were watching her from the governess' shadow, where they appeared to be playing a game with her.

Jasper was lounging at the window with Isabelle on his lap. She smiled quickly and straightened from her slump. She could not dwell on her problems with the children's father. They had once been sensitive to her moods, and her time with them was too precious to waste.

Jasper strolled over with Isabelle, nodding and grinning like he was party to a great secret. "Finally, you're here."

"Yes, for now," she said.

"The worst is over," he promised, handing Isabelle to her, then tickling her tummy and making her laugh. "You've seen your husband and survived. It will be easy to resume your life with us."

"For the next thirty days only," she told him.

"What?"

Laura explained the bargain she'd just made with the duke.

"What nonsense! You belong here with us. Nash should be the one to leave if he doesn't want you here," Jasper protested.

But he was mad to think she could want to stay at Ravenswood. There was no going back now. Too much bad blood between them. Too many days spent alone, even before she'd left him.

But she could smile because the duke decreed she could be with her children whenever she wanted over the next thirty days. Spending an hour with her husband was a minor detriment to her happiness over that.

Jasper exchanged a long glance with Mrs.

Radcliffe. "Sophie and I are undecided if we should leave the estate now or wait."

"Do not stay longer than you want to on my account. I knew my reception would not be a warm one."

"Well. Not from certain quarters perhaps, but from mine, it is the opposite. Might I embrace you, sister dear?" Jasper asked hesitantly.

She frowned at him.

"I have several years' worth of Christmastime good cheer and birthday affection to share. Perhaps I could limit it to one long embrace, so it is not embarrassing to either of us," Jasper teased.

She sighed. "Very well," she whispered, and let herself be pulled into his arms. But she did not allow such sentimentality to continue for very long. In looks, Jasper could remind her of Nash, but the differences in their natures were vast.

The former governess drew closer when she was released. "You must be tired, my lady," Sophie suggested hesitantly.

"Perhaps I am a little." She jiggled Isabelle on her hip. "They grow so fast, don't they?"

"Always," the woman agreed. "Would you allow me to help you with her?"

"The duke might not like that. He has decreed only myself and my husband should have the care of them now."

"I am sure he didn't intend to exclude family

from playing with the children or holding Isabelle, because we are inordinately fond of them all," Jasper warned.

Laura considered Jasper and the woman he would marry, and then nodded. Someone here had to care about Isabelle and the boys when she was gone. Why not allow Jasper and Mrs. Radcliffe to build the bond with Isabelle, who would need them for love and comfort.

Laura already trusted Jasper to look after her daughter when she couldn't. And she was more tired than she expected to be. Confronting Nash had been nerve-wracking.

Sophie swept the girl from her arms and spoke to her, only to plop her on the floor beside Thomas the next moment. "Please watch over your sister, Thomas."

"I won't let her out of my sight," he promised, parroting his father. But his glance took Laura in, too.

Laura winced. She'd had no chance to explain to Thomas that she was going away. It had all happened so quickly.

He would have been too young to understand why she'd been so weak and sickly and getting worse through no fault of her own.

Laura let out a shaky breath, but her anxiety eased at seeing her children sitting together at play and seemingly happy in each other's company. She wanted to always imagine them so.

Jasper led her to sit near the window. "Since we never had tea in the drawing room, I have asked for it to be brought here instead."

"You've always been the most considerate of the family, Jasper," she told him.

"I take after the only sister I ever had, who taught me more about kindness and patience than anyone in this family ever could."

She shook her head and grinned reluctantly. "You were always the most likely to flatter without cause, too."

"No. No. You deserve every praise I can heap on your head right now." He leaned closer. "You did not have an easy time making a place for yourself in this family. Despite my brother's silence, I'm sure he was happy to see you, though."

"I'm sure you don't know what you're talking about yet again," she countered, looking across the room at Sophie. The woman was listening. So were the boys and she lowered her voice to a whisper. "Nash doesn't care about me, and he never did."

"I know my brother. He cared for no woman *but* you," Jasper promised.

Laura winced. "He didn't miss me or need me. He got his heir and spare."

"In the beginning of your marriage, Nash always headed upstairs the moment he returned to the estate. We often teased him about that but Father chided him for it. Demanding attention first, as he did with all of us. He'd send us off for any odd reason so we were hardly ever together here at the same time. When we realized you were gone, he forbid us writing to alert Nash or looking for you ourselves. On the day Nash finally did return, Father let him discover you missing on his own."

"The late duke would have enjoyed his son's humiliation. Knowing everything and ordering Nash about made him feel powerful." She imagined that easily, because she'd heard it herself. The duke taunting his second son, telling him how capricious women could be. How unstable and troublesome Laura was becoming. In the end, she'd proved him right.

"Admittedly, Nash's steps grew slower in the years after you left him, but I'm sure he still hoped to find you had returned home in his absence all this time."

She shook away the hope so at odds with the reality. "So you will marry Mrs. Radcliffe?"

"Yes," he admitted. "We were thrown together while the duke was away and found we had more in common than not. The plans we're making might exclude us from proper society in the end, but we have each other and the duke's blessing."

"I'm glad you found someone you can care for. It is good to know each's dreams and support them."

"Sophie will inherit a pleasure house," Jasper whispered, sounding rather proud.

Laura choked and glanced at Sophie. "The establishment where my husband met her?"

Sophie came close. "He met me nearly dying there. My babe lost too soon."

Laura winced, glancing at Jasper, wondering how he bore that news. Yet he only smiled at Sophie with absolute love in his eyes and reached out for her hand to squeeze it.

Jasper Sweet had chosen a truly unconventional bride indeed, a ruined woman, and surprisingly so had Nash, but she had to admit it might be a better match for Jasper instead.

Sophie was just the sort of woman the late duke would have refused to permit any match with though. She was surprised the current duke had allowed such a thing. "I'm very sorry for your loss, Mrs. Radcliffe. Children are a blessing."

"Sophie, please. Since we are to be almost sisters for a while. Your husband's offer of employment saved me from becoming a lady of the night. I was an orphan, and I had nothing and no one to turn to besides my new friends at the brothel. Your husband was never really my particular friend."

"Not like I have become, she means," Jasper hastened to assure her with a wink. "Sophie has been a model of decorum since her arrival, which was why we did not get along so well at first."

"Not for a long time," Sophie added, offering him a sweet smile, and then she threw a cheeky smile at Laura. "Not until you left Isabelle on his bed. I thought him just another heartless rake until then."

"It was the sheer panic in my voice that finally softened her heart toward me," Jasper claimed, grinning deeply. "I owe my current state of happiness all to you, dear sister, and little Isabelle, for casting up her accounts all over my favorite waistcoat. Sophie took pity on me then and our friendship grew."

She sighed at the spectacle her daughter must have made. "I apologize for the inconvenience of leaving her on your bed. My visit was meant to be brief but the house was awash with strangers and I discovered Nash away with the duke too. I had to leave her with someone in the family. And since you were always so good with your younger cousins, I trusted you to take charge of her and keep her safe until her father returned."

"I'm glad you trust me. You can trust us all, you know."

She exhaled shakily. "When will you be married?"

"Not until we reach London, and the sooner the better, although I think Algernon wishes to host the wedding breakfast here. He quite enjoyed surprising cousin Amity with her own wedding breakfast earlier in the year."

"So your cousin married at last? I assume it was the great match your cousin George told everyone to expect from his side of the family. Only someone from the finest aristocratic ranks and rich would have gained his approval."

"George is not pleased, the pig. Amity ruined herself to get away from a bad match and then fell in love later. Algernon smoothed things over, so no one said a word against the match, really."

"His first manipulation as duke?" she asked. "I gather he's well on his way to emulating your father now."

"Well, if Amity was his victim, then he's a gift for making women happy. I've never seen a couple more in love than Amity and our friend, Mr. Roman Crawford." Jasper grinned up at Sophie and brought her hand to his lips. "Until now, of course. No one could be happier than the pair of us."

Laura averted her eyes at the overt display of affection between the pair. Jasper had always been so different to Nash. Outgoing and flirtatious. Clearly, he would be an affectionate husband toward Sophie. They stood a chance of being happy together if that continued. Happier than she and Nash had ever had the opportunity to be under the old duke's thumb.

She bit her tongue as the tea tray arrived, carried in by a servant she didn't recognize. It was a reminder that things could change at Ravenswood, but a warning that nothing lasted here either. Laura had to look to the future to find hope, or at least peace now.

She would be divorced soon and then...well, life would be so very different from what it was supposed to have been.

Laura had to take charge of her life now, so she poured tea for the newly engaged pair and wished them every happiness.

"I'm sure my older brother will break out the good stuff soon enough so we can celebrate properly together," Jasper warned.

"I'm sure he will," she murmured. "Enjoy your celebration."

"We'll enjoy the celebration together," Jasper said, giving her a pointed look. "Please."

"I'm sure I'm not wanted, unless awkward silences and scowls are what you seek," Laura said, and then settled back in the window seat with her cup of tea. She could not imagine any merriment where her husband was sitting opposite her. She'd suffered through enough formal dinners at Ravenswood to want to avoid future ones where she still could not speak her mind.

"I'd like you there with us, too," Sophie added, wringing her hands. "I've rarely joined the duke for celebrations. I'd appreciate your support and a woman's company in the drawing room afterward, so I'm not all alone."

Laura winced. She understood how intimidating this family could be, even when you'd been groomed to marry into it. But Sophie had Jasper to rely upon. He would stand up for her and remain by her side in a way Nash never had for her. "They hardly ever insult you to your face. The knives come out later."

Jasper sighed. "It's not like that here anymore," he promised. "Just you wait and see."

Laura shook her head, unable to believe that. "You will have a very happy match, I think, if you always support each other."

"I plan to," Jasper assured her, jumping to his feet to take up Sophie's hand and press kisses to the back of it.

Laura watched the exchange with growing respect for the match. Sophie already held her future husband in the palm of her hand and he seemed to enjoy being kept there. She had quickly achieved what many women dream of for the whole of their unhappy married lives.

Laura certainly had never achieved so much with Nash. She could begrudge no one a better courtship than hers had been. "Very well. I will join you to celebrate your engagement if I am still here."

She glanced down at herself. Her gown was not exactly acceptable for a formal celebratory dinner, but she was done trying to please members of this family. If her husband complained about her appearance, too bad. She had brought nothing finer with her.

She moved away from the betrothed couple and knelt on the floor near her children. She did not interrupt, just watched them play together. They seemed to get along well so far. Eventually, Isabelle grew tired of playing peek-a-boos and came crawling over, asking without words to be held.

Laura hesitated a moment before picking up her child. Soon she would not have the chance to hold her close. It was a heavy price she would pay for her freedom in the end. Laura had expected to leave with nothing tonight but the clothes on her back until the duke had insisted she stay. She would remain for her daughter's sake. But more than mothering, Isabelle needed the security and protection only her father could provide.

Another servant appeared. An older woman Laura remembered. However she could hardly looked her in the eye now though. Probably afraid the duke would punish her for her help all those years ago. "His Grace has asked me to attend to you, Lady Sweet."

"I can manage on my own," she promised, deciding she would keep her involvement a secret.

"That is what he said you would say. Your room has been prepared, a bath drawn, and your gowns are being pressed as we speak. I am to help you disrobe, bathe, and to dress afterward."

Laura squinted at the servant. "How do you have any of my gowns to press?"

"His Grace ordered your single trunk brought to Ravenswood from your family estate," the servant claimed. "If you will follow me now, the water is growing cold."

Although surprised by this turn of events, she dared not let it show. The duke had eyes and ears everywhere. Just like the last one had. She would have to be careful.

"If the duke expects me to sit down to dinner tonight, he will have to accept me the way I am. I prefer to spend the time I have with my children."

"He thought you would say that, too, and he said to tell you that you are excused from dining with him tonight. He suggested you make yourself at home, and that the children might enjoy a bath in your chambers after you are done with the water."

Isabelle had always enjoyed bath time. So had her sons when they were much younger. They looked at Laura now, clearly excited about the idea of taking a bath in her chambers, their breaths held, their eyes alight with barely hidden excitement.

She quickly nodded. "Very well. Bring them in five minutes."

"Twenty minutes," the servant countered with a quick, apologetic smile for the room. "Your hair has grown quite long while you were gone, my lady. It will take more time to wash properly now."

Laura knew that was quite true and sighed a second time. "Very well. Twenty minutes."

"I'll fetch the children as soon as you are decent," the woman promised. "They usually take their supper at five o'clock in the nursery. His Grace expected that you would wish to join them."

"I would."

The woman smiled. But Laura knew she had been maneuvered into doing exactly what the Duke of Ravenswood wanted her to do.

Laura stood, handing Isabelle off to Jasper, who appeared eager to hold his niece again.

"Until tomorrow, sister."

"I suppose so," she said, and then followed the servant out of the room.

The woman hurried her down to the floor below and along the hall to a chamber she'd never expected or wanted to stand in again.

Her old chamber appeared unchanged, despite the nearly two years she'd been away from Ravenswood. The curtains were still blue, the windows tall, and the bed was...

She gulped. The bed and coverlet were exactly the same. She had spent every night of her marriage in that bed. The nights with Nash were the only happy memories she had of her marriage besides the time she'd spent with her children.

She turned her back on the vast expanse and the past firmly.

In pride of place before the fire was a huge steaming copper tub already filled with perfumed water. Laura sighed and drew closer as the servant added another steaming kettle of water. Rose petal had been scattered on the surface, just the way she'd always liked it. "I did miss this tub."

"It's ready. Can I help you undress, my lady?"

"No. I can manage," Laura said, slipping out of her own garments, letting them fall to the floor. She wasted no time getting into the hot water to hide her old unsightly scars, not that this servant would be surprised by their existence since she'd seen them made fresh. She was eager to partake of the only indulgent luxury she'd ever truly enjoyed at Ravenswood, and twenty minutes hardly seemed long enough.

The long tub held enough hot water to cover her completely. She sank into it and then completely under the surface, holding her breath for as long as she could manage.

When her head broke the surface, she felt unbearably weary. Yet her uncertainty was gone and hope for a brighter, happier tomorrow lay ahead.

Nash would not fight her about the divorce. Perhaps coming home to Ravenswood now hadn't been such a terrible decision. She had more freedom this time than she'd had before. She would revel in the novelty and be herself for the first time ever. If Nash didn't like it, he could go to the devil, too.

She turned to the servant. "I want to thank you for your assistance."

"I'm relieved to know you survived, my lady," the woman whispered back, eyes darting to the door. "You did not deserve what was done to you."

"No I did not," Laura answered and her jaw clenched in remembrance.

CHAPTER FOUR

"THAT'S THE LAST OF THEM," Nash promised, dropping a huge bundle of books on the library reading table for his brother the next morning. He was still annoyed Algernon had harassed him to bring them back. There were more important things to deal with, such as discussing a wife who didn't want to be one anymore.

He had not slept well last night, knowing Laura was near.

Although he was not pleased to see Laura return, he could not ignore what felt like a cataclysmic shift in the atmosphere at Ravenswood, and in himself, overnight.

He'd passed three maids who had smiled at him and then giggled when they'd passed him by. Even the valet he shared with his brother had been humming to himself.

Nash had a wife again, and a young daughter now too, but he did not hum or smile or giggle about the novelty. He did not know what to do about either, particularly his daughter.

Laura had seduced him, and he could not understand why.

He remembered that night more and more, though. Intimacy had been good between them. Urgent, hot. He had not restrained himself very much, and Laura had hardly been cold toward him, either.

He could not ignore Laura now, but neither did he wish to face her again so soon without having a plan first. His mistake, his indiscretion, had come back to haunt him and made him considerably discomforted. How could he not have recognized Laura in the dark? They had been married five years by then.

He thought he'd known her and her body well. He could only blame extreme intoxication for that level of blindness. He'd put up no resistance when their exchange turned passionate almost immediately. But some part of him must have recognized his wife.

He glanced about the piles of books scattered here and there in the library and focused on small things he understood. Those tasks he could complete and feel good about.

But behind him were great voids. His study was cold and emptier and had echoed oddly with the sound of his solitary footsteps. He would have to adjust to that as well later, but first he would help bring the untidiness here to order.

He picked up a stack of books, read the spines, and looked about for where they should belong.

"Nash, I prefer to put everything back in its proper place in the library myself. But should you need to refer to these books again, you can, of course, always find them here," Algernon promised. "However, I do doubt you'll have time for any extensive reading."

"Why?"

"You will have your hands full with your wife and children. And with them is where you should be already, by the way. Leave this to me to put right and get going."

"But—"

"No, brother. I don't need any help to put a handful of books away."

"It's not a handful. There are dozens," he protested.

Algernon looked over his shoulder at the work ahead and, although his eyes widened when he realized the number, he eventually shrugged. "I can manage this small feat unaided, I assure you."

Algernon had always wanted his help in the past so he did not argue the point further. Algernon was not just his brother, but his best friend, too. He did not like them disagreeing about anything.

"It was private research. The divorce," Nash murmured, shuffling his feet. "I didn't want to involve you until the time was right."

"Nothing has ever been private between us before, brother," Algernon reminded him, adding volumes back to the upper shelves and sliding down the ladder again to pick up another stack. "That's why we have rarely ever argued over the years. But you should consider who you make your confidant in the future. I recommend you talk about your plans for the future with your wife instead of me. They will affect her most of all."

As a boy, he and Algernon had leaned on each other. Confiding, confessing and plotting ways to escape their father's control and defy his demands for their absolute obedience. They had watched over their younger brothers together, protecting them as best they could. To hear that he should not confide in Algernon anymore was a kick in the gut. No one understood him better than his own brother.

Nash turned on his heel and stalked off, confused and hurt by Algernon pushing him away and siding with Laura, now of all times. An unmarried man did not really understand the confusion that came with being a husband to such a woman.

He entered a much smaller chamber than he'd taken over, a room tucked away between two larger chambers on the far side of the house, and slammed the door shut. It was quiet here. Private. No one ever bothered him here, and he inhaled the familiar atmosphere, expecting it to be a balm to his senses. But with the absence of his favorite books his satisfaction ebbed.

He'd furnished the tiny room himself over the years with the discards from other parts of the house that Father had not wanted or noticed missing. His only comfort in recent years, when he'd finally had a moment to himself, was getting lost in the pages of his favorite volumes from the library.

It would be tedious to have to find them again, and less pleasing to read in another room, one where everyone came and went so often.

Nash liked the quiet, his out of the way room, and the jumble of mismatched furniture usually smothered by books he'd hoarded. Now there were bare surfaces and dust lines showing where books had once rested. The pair of wingback chairs, one old and one new. The battered oak desk standing between two windows was held up at the back by blocks of wood, its surface far too bare. He'd no excuse to stay in this room for long now.

He swiped away a patch of dust on a side table and grimaced. He would need to put a servant to work in here soon to tidy things up again. He'd spent much of the last two years alone in this room while pretending it hadn't hurt that his wife had left him.

But it did.

Now he felt doubly rejected.

He groaned and swiped at another patch of dust angrily. The room had been closed up for weeks, so he opened a window a crack to let in some fresh air and glanced outside.

Beyond the window, he saw shapes moving through the gardens. He squinted at them, but quickly realized that it was not gardeners at work.

Three figures...no, four. A woman with a babe on her hip and two small boys were running away from the manor.

Laura was leaving—again—and taking his children this time!

Panicked, he flung the window wide and jumped out in pursuit.

Laura and his children had a good head start and were headed toward her family estate on foot. Nash had to run to catch up with them before they disappeared out of sight.

He caught up with them on the maze path. "Where the hell do you think you're going?"

Laura, wearing a different gown of deep green from when he'd last seen her, barely turned to look at him when she answered. "I thought it obvious."

"Take them back inside," he ordered.

Her chin rose. "No."

Nash caught her arm to halt her. "You dare defy me?"

"Oh, I dare." Her gaze slowly lifted to his. "I'm no meek lamb to the slaughter anymore."

He pulled her closer. "Meek was never a word I ever used to describe you."

"Just as well," she quipped with a haughty shake of her head. She looked down at where he clung to her arm. "Take your hand off me."

Unfortunately, he had difficulty unlocking his fingers immediately. Despite the long sleeves of her gown, Laura was warm and soft under his fingers and touching her was like a fire in his veins. It was a reaction he'd felt before with her. Once, he'd thought that meant something.

He held her gaze, completely at a loss for what to say now that he had hold of her, and utterly confused by what he was feeling. Was it fury, despair, pride or—even worse—need?

He could *not* need her. Not again.

He let her go, but slowly.

Laura stepped back immediately, turning her face away and calling out, "Children, where are you?"

"We're over here," Thomas called back.

Liam giggled.

Laura turned the corner to go around the maze. "Where?"

"Here," they called.

Nash shook his head and rushed after Laura, only to find her at a stop beside the maze hedge. The children were nowhere in sight.

"I must have missed the entrance," Laura muttered, barging past him in search of the way in. "Where are they?"

"There is no entrance on this side," he warned. "The maze changed after you left and the few gardeners who remain haven't clipped the hedges since well before Father died. It's grown thick again. Many of the paths inside have disappeared entirely, I imagine."

He followed Laura, who seemed on the verge of panic now, frantically peering through the hedge.

"They can't be too far in. Children," he called out, "come to the sound of my voice."

There was a whispered conversation on the other side of the hedge, and then Thomas answered. "We can't find the way out. What are we going to do?"

Nash groaned at the obvious panic in his youngest son's voice, but he saw a flash of color from Liam's blue coat through the foliage. "Stay right where you are. I'm coming."

Nash ripped at the hedge barehanded, creating a new opening in the wall of greenery to get to his children. It wasn't easy; the hedge was very old and the branches had thorns that cut into his hands, but eventually he made a large enough hole that the pair could be pulled through.

Liam looked about to cry, and Thomas appeared highly embarrassed. Nash pushed his arms through and shoved back one side far enough that he could see them. He used his feet to push back the other side to make it even larger for the boys. "Come through now and be careful you don't scratch yourselves."

The boys squeezed over him and, once on the other side, dusted themselves off without being asked.

Nash jumped out of the gap, and the hedge mostly closed behind him again. He glanced down at his hands, which were now stinging and bleeding.

The boys looked up at Nash, then at Laura—and then burst into tears.

Nash, troubled by their tears, gently shushed them. Tears solved nothing. He bent down to their level and murmured, "No more running into the maze without me or your uncles."

Laura heaved a sigh. "I didn't know the maze was not fit for playing in anymore or I'd never have suggested it."

"No, you know nothing about us or this place anymore," he bit out, giving her the set down she deserved for placing the children in harm's way. The maze was not a place for unattended children. "Next time, ask me before you think to leave Ravenswood."

"I wasn't leaving Ravenswood. We were just going outside to play," she protested.

"Well, what was I to think, given how you fled us last time? Go back inside and wait for me in the nursery."

Laura's hand curled into fists around Isabelle. "You couldn't even let them have a day away from their studies to be with me?"

"They were already with you in the nursery."

Laura held his gaze for a long moment. "Have you any idea how to be spontaneous?"

"Clearly you think I don't," he answered, then remembered the children were watching them fight. Their daughter was too young to understand, but the boys surely would understand anger. He started them back toward the palace, encouraging them to run if they wanted to.

He nodded approvingly as Thomas challenged Liam to a race, just as Algernon had done with Nash when they were boys.

"Now the boys are gone, you can cease being stoic and show me your injuries," Laura demanded, juggling Isabelle and extending one gloved hand.

Surprised by her concern, he let her see the result of her ill-considered decision. Her touch was light, impersonal, as she inspected his skin and each irritating gash.

Nash caught the scent of Laura's perfume in the air, and he shuddered slightly.

"I did not mean for you to get hurt," Laura whispered.

But Nash felt no real pain anymore.

Laura had always smelled sweet because of the scented oils and rose petals she added to her bathwater. The combination of woman and perfume had always been soothing to his senses, and arousing.

"Some of these will need proper cleaning. Do they hurt badly?"

He shook his head. Nothing had ever hurt when Laura touched him.

He studied her, unable to tear his eyes away, now that they were so close. Her cheeks flushed with soft color and her lips were pink and pouted. The thought of her in scented hot water, made him tremble again. He'd never dared interrupt her bath, but had imagined her so many times that way.

Laura noticed the shake of his hand and lifted her gaze to his.

Desire flooded him, nearly knocking him off his feet. He wanted to reach out and pull Laura into his arms and let her hair down. Clutch the long strands in his fist as he used to do when they made love and feel her soft, scented limbs slide against his as he kissed her.

He inched closer and inhaled a deeper lungful. Isabelle, however, was held between them, and he could do nothing more than look.

Laura suddenly sniffed the air and her nose wrinkled with distaste instead of the pleasure he felt. "Someone needs changing again," she murmured.

Nash shook his head, thoughts of lovemaking fading fast as he realized his daughter had soiled her garments.

"Have your valet soak your hand in warm water and a few drops of lavender, if he has any," Laura told him, putting distance between them at last.

"I can do that myself," he promised. "I'm more practiced in applying herbs and bandages than anyone at the estate, after all."

"Yes, of course you would think that." She sighed. "Well, tend to yourself for all I care, and if you insist we're to be confined to the nursery to play, then you'll also be the one to empty the chamber pots. I will take care of our daughter. You, the boys."

"We've servants for that," he argued.

"Oh, no we don't. Not anymore. Not during the day. The duke issued specific instructions for what the servants can or cannot do with the children. We are solely responsible for our children's care now. That includes bathing and changing, feeding and cleaning up after them. Do you know how to do any of that?"

"Of course I do," he assured her. He just never had to before. He'd had Sophie, and before that, the old nursery maid had taken care of the boys since they were born. Laura hadn't needed to lift a finger since the day their children had arrived. "I suspect I know more about managing a household than you ever could."

"Then you would be wrong. As you've always been about me," she whispered. "But I've no desire to waste my breath and time by arguing with you."

She forged ahead with a violent shake of her head before he could stop her. He followed her immediately, but she went directly to where the children were crouched down to look at something near the ground. "Come along, children. Leave the poor insect be. We'll return to the nursery and you can show me how clever you've become."

"I'm the cleverest boy," Liam announced proudly, looking at Laura with excitement shining in his eyes. "Miss Sophie told me so."

"Well, I'm sure she's correct," Laura promised him, gazing upon their youngest son with a keen interest, though he must barely remember her. Thomas held himself apart from Laura. He watched her carefully but seemed unable or unwilling to let her too close.

Laura faced an uphill battle to reconnect with their sons after all this time away. They had been much too young when she left to remember much about her now.

They headed toward Ravenswood ahead of Nash, talking together and giving him no part in the conversation about what they would do next that afternoon.

He watched Laura particularly as they moved closer to the palace. Noticed that she hugged Isabelle tighter than ever as she moved into the shadow cast by the house.

She hated to be here. She had returned only for the sake of securing their daughter's future and her position in the family when she was gone.

The child had *him* to watch over her now, of course. Nash would never neglect his own offspring. But he could admit to himself that perhaps he had neglected his wife. Becoming so wrapped up in protecting the needs of the family at large, particularly his brothers, had meant she'd been temporarily set to one side. But he'd truly believed Laura would benefit in the end.

Just seeing her again had stirred up so many memories...her complaints, and her familiar presence that soothed him when her body was so close at night. Laura had kept him enthralled long after she'd left.

Father had thought him a softhearted fool and tried to strip him of sentiment as a boy. He'd thought the old man had failed, but maybe he had actually succeeded. Even though Father was gone and no longer a source of conflict, Nash had trouble seeing how he could have done things any differently.

He'd driven her away, perhaps unconsciously. She had been impossible to live with and unhappy. Now things were to change further between them, with the divorce to come.

Instead of the peace he expected, he now had fresh disagreements to mull over and dissect when he could not sleep.

He could not pretend that Laura had felt anything for him, either. She had requested a divorce, too, and the closed door that connected their bedchambers would stay shut for the next thirty days.

For the sake of his sanity, he hoped Algernon would change his mind about supporting the divorce they both wanted. Otherwise, this could very well be the most frustrating month of his entire life.

CHAPTER FIVE

LAURA GLANCED OVER HER SHOULDER, unaccustomed to having her husband nearby for so long. But Nash was still there, following her about today, revealing no emotion.

Usually, he would have run off the minute she turned her back. She'd seen no sign of him yesterday after her bath or even heard him in his chambers later that evening.

After they married, after he'd left her bed, he rarely seemed to give her a second thought until the dinner hour or later that night. He was in for a rude shock if he thought she would ever welcome his company now, though.

It was only the current duke's order that he remain by her side—fulfilling a duty imposed on him, rather than harboring any genuine desire to be near her or their children. She had the distinct impression he feared she had been about to run off with them today though.

She would not do that to them. She could not support three children or offer them a home of their own. No. They had to stay with their father, no matter how much it pained her. Perhaps he would change for them in the years ahead. She hoped he could.

But their entire marriage had been years of loneliness for *her*. Nash had forever been a dutiful son to the late Duke of Ravenswood and loyal brother to his three siblings. He did what he was told, and he was still doing that for the new duke, too.

She didn't expect him to change for her anymore. He'd never put her first or been the devoted husband she'd so hoped for. He'd shown his true colors last year at the masquerade ball, when she'd discovered the gold band she'd placed on his ring finger on their wedding day had been removed.

It was still missing.

That made things crystal clear. Why should she feel guilty for wanting a formal separation when he'd left her, too?

It didn't matter that Laura had spent another night with him since fleeing the estate. Nash had displayed no hesitation to be unfaithful to her at that masquerade ball.

Laura had known all along that she was with Nash and, at that time, she'd been feeling foolishly sentimental. When she'd seen him standing apart from everyone, she'd had second thoughts about leaving him. She had considered a return to their marriage, but had wanted to know what she would face.

But then he'd seen her, and everyone else in that masquerade had faded away. Her good sense, too. He'd crooked his finger, and she'd almost run across the ballroom to reach him.

Laura had lost the fight with her need for his arms wrapped around, and when he'd held her close and kissed her soundly, she was swept back to those long-ago heated nights in her bed. She had done one last selfish act.

She glanced down at her daughter now and sighed. Look at what sentimentality and desire had done to her. Another babe. Not that she could ever regretted Isabelle's existence.

A daughter was a gift, a treasure. But the pregnancy had made her future more difficult to face, especially so when neighbors had asked where the child had come from.

A return to Ravenswood had been inevitable, to request the recognition that should have been Isabelle's all along.

She wished she had the funds to raise Isabelle and the boys away from here. But she had already taken as much charity as she dared take from anyone. She had so wanted to see her children grow up and have the life they deserved. The boys had already grown so tall and sturdy. They had not suffered for her absence. She was glad of that.

Yet the issue that still concerned her with divorcing Nash was the difficulty she might have in seeing her children in the future. She did not want to walk away from this marriage without some assurances, in writing, that she could remain part of their lives in some fashion.

She turned back to her husband, causing Nash to stop suddenly, almost on top of her. She looked up into his eyes and her breath caught again. She still was affected by him. But she could not afford to make another mistake and wisely took a step back. "I think we can both agree the duke is in error in believing our children need both of us every moment of every day until he decides to support the divorce."

Nash frowned, still towering over her. "Is that right?"

"Well, of course I'm right," she insisted, holding her ground. She could not let her husband intimidate her.

He bent slightly toward her and held her gaze. "What do you propose we do about this error of his?"

"Well, you go about your usual business

while I go about mine," she suggested, momentarily disconcerted by the drop of his gaze to her lips.

He wet his own. "I'm curious to know what you think *is* my business?"

She cleared her throat and waved her hand about in the air, fighting the pull of attraction she should not be feeling around Nash. It was easier to be near him when they were arguing. "I hardly know or care to find out now. Whatever you normally do while the sun shines? Something involving the duke, no doubt."

He pursed his lips, clearly considering the idea. But then he frowned again. "What will you be doing today?"

She smiled. "Getting reacquainted with my sons."

His eyes dipped to Isabelle's wriggling arms. "What of Isabelle?"

"She will be with me, of course," she promised.

As soon as she finished speaking, he nodded and took the child from her. He turned Isabelle around to face him, holding her in midair and studying her face. "She has your eyes."

"Yes," Laura agreed, reaching for the girl.

Nash ignored her, turning Isabelle this way and that as he studied her. "My ears."

Her gaze was drawn to the ears in discussion. He was right. "Yes."

He sighed and drew Isabelle against his chest. "The boys have *your* ears, not mine."

"They have your eyes," Laura admitted.

"It is interesting, is it not? I wonder which of us she will take after when she is fully grown."

"Does it matter?"

"No, it doesn't. But I hope she takes after you more than me." He handed Isabelle back to her. "You're much easier on the eye."

She did not know what to say to that and fussed with straightening their daughter's smock instead. Nash stepped back, and she sighed in relief. It was much too late for him to compliment her looks. "Goodbye then."

"No. I *will* escort you both to the nursery first," he murmured.

Laura needed no escort, least of all his. She had not forgotten how to navigate the palace's many corridors and hidden staircases. Wishing to return to a combative footing, she scoffed, "I know where the nursery is, but I wonder if you have forgotten?"

"I have certainly visited the nursery more often than you have in the last few years," he complained.

"Well, that is something positive to come from my leaving. When we were married, you never ventured to the third floor if you could help it. You were too busy chasing your father around."

"I chase no one," he hissed, eyes flashing with anger now. "My family appreciates my efforts, unlike someone I could name."

"I will never understand why your wife and children had to come second to an estate that will never be yours," she hissed. "But by all means, go find your brother and make him proud of your dedication."

He sucked in a sharp breath. "Madam, let me make one thing clear: everything I have ever done is for you and our children, and we are still married, so I will escort you anywhere I damn well please."

She smiled, glad she'd pushed him enough to become angry with her at last. "Not married for much longer if I have my way. The duke is unhinged if he believes we belong anywhere near each other. You can even tell him I said that when you see him."

"I assure you the duke is of sound mind," he said, though his expression might have finally shown just a hint of doubt about that. It was brief but easily swept away by his pride in his family. "However, he likes to have his own way."

"As do you, but you won't have it in all things this time with me," she told him.

His brows drew together. "What do you mean by that?"

Isabelle fussed. Laura bounced the child on her hip, knowing she had to end this conversation soon and put Isabelle down to sleep. But she wanted to leave Nash in no doubt where their marriage was headed. Separation in all things, especially in the bedchamber. "I do not crave your attention anymore."

He blinked, and his eyes narrowed.

Nash was going to be difficult and pretend he did not understand her meaning. But then, he had always done that when he didn't like what he heard. He was stubborn. Well, she could be stubborn, too. And when she proved too vexing, no doubt he'd scurry off to where he normally spent his days and leave her alone with the boys.

Yet he continued to stare at her. "I never knew that."

"Knew what?"

"That you craved my attention," he drew close, and his hand rose toward her.

She stepped back out of range. "Dear God, you are years too late for that. Many wives want their husbands in the beginning. For companionship. For conversation."

"For intimacy, too. I gave you that."

"Nights, and nothing more."

His jaw set stubbornly for a moment. "I gave you every spare moment I had to give."

She laughed darkly. "Well, it wasn't enough for me then, and it certainly isn't what I desire now. I urge you to do all you can to pursue our divorce with or without the duke's support. We don't belong together. Get yourself an easily impressed mistress who will be satisfied with your fleeting attention. But never burden another lady with an offer of marriage. You'll only make them miserable. One wife so neglected should be enough for any man in his lifetime."

Nash took a pace toward her again, his expression incredulous and his nostrils flaring in anger. "You go too far, madam."

Perhaps she had, but their marriage had hardened her. She'd no intention of crossing the threshold into his room or welcoming him to join her in hers. He'd never been forceful about claiming his marital rights. But he had always come to her with one thing on his mind. Sex followed by immediate sleep. It had never been to talk. "I will go as far as I need to secure what's mine."

"And what would that be?"

"Peace and the funds I was promised in the marriage contract, should the marriage fail."

But clearly her demands brought out the beast in him. Nash seized her by both arms, and his touch sent an unexpected surge of excitement trembling through her entire being.

His eyes locked on hers, and her nether regions quivered with an annoying urge to yield to him yet again. She narrowed her eyes at him, fighting that old feeling with all her might. "Let me go."

"You are my wife."

"Not for much longer." After so many years married to him, she did not really fear his displeasure. She wanted it, so he would give her what she needed. Freedom.

Nash however, drew her even closer, trapping Isabelle between their bodies. "Mine for now," he whispered.

His head began to lower, his intent clear and she panicked and struggled in earnest. "If you're expecting a warm welcome, you will not find it. Quite the opposite. I will not endure intimate relations with you again."

He recoiled as if she'd slapped him. "Endure?"

"Yes, endure," she insisted, trying to make her body believe that was how it had been between them back then. His attentions had been tender and vigorous and at the time, she'd fooled herself into believing he cared.

"I never forced you to do anything you didn't

thoroughly enjoy or beg me for more of," Nash argued, keeping her close.

That was true, unfortunately.

She pushed him away with one hand, noticing that he was still as heavy and solid as she remembered. "That woman is long gone. I am done with you, Nash."

She turned her gaze down to Isabelle even as she turned away from Nash, fighting the trembling he caused as she left him standing where he was in the courtyard.

Laura had loved Nash, but she could not permit such foolish sentiment to get the better of her still. She would only be hurt again.

They both had asked for an end to their marriage. It was over.

Passion was a poor substitute for a genuine friendship, an actual marriage. And he'd never once tried for that. Nash had kept her on the outside, separated from his real life in the family, a plaything for when he had a spare moment in the evenings.

She had deserved to be far more than that to him. To anyone. If Nash had ever really needed her in his life, he should have run away with her when she'd suggested it.

Laura hadn't really made herself hard to find. Another member of the family had found her in less than a month—and then offered her the means to stay hidden from Nash and the rest of the Ravenswood family.

She'd refused at first, of course, suspecting she'd be betrayed and delivered back to Ravenswood. But no one had come in the end and Nash had carried on with his life without a backward glance. She understood her real value to him had only ever been the size of her dowry and her fertile womb. He'd taken everything from her and given back nothing but misery.

By the time Laura reached the stairs, Nash was by her side again, hand sliding around her waist to support her as she began to ascend, carrying Isabelle. Although she tried to avoid his touch, carrying Isabelle up the steep flight was a little difficult in long skirts. She managed the first flight in the end, but at the second, Nash snatched Isabelle from her.

Although she called out for him to stop, he climbed the steeper flight of stairs two at a time, reaching the top where the nursery was well ahead of her. She cursed him under her breath and hurried up as fast as she could, holding up her long skirts and using the handrail.

Nash had waited for her at the top and handed Isabelle back immediately. "In the future, please ask for help with her. She wriggles a great deal."

"I have always managed on my own with her," Laura complained.

"My point is you don't have to. You may not have servants to help, but you still have me," he said. "Despite your low opinion of me, I wouldn't want you to fall and be hurt."

Laura met his gaze. An awkward silence descended over them. "Excuse me."

She hurried away, and when she slipped through the nursery doorway, she was glad that he did not follow her anymore.

CHAPTER SIX

SEVERAL HOURS LATER, Nash was still deeply troubled that Laura could speak so dismissively of their marriage. No, it had not been perfect. He'd had so many demands on his time back then. But to hear her claim the hours they'd spent together at night amounted to next to nothing was ridiculous. That was an insult to his honor and the existence of their offspring.

Laura had told him she wanted a dozen children, and he'd made sure that she'd been well cared for, able to bring their first two children to term as easily as possible. He'd watched over her carefully, and when it quickly became apparent he could not be with her every moment of the day, he'd assigned staff to that role.

He trudged up the steep stairs to the nursery after waiting enough time for their tempers to cool again. He would not be dismissed by her so easily. He could not avoid Laura.

He had nothing else to do anymore, too. The duke had taken all his favorite books away and did not require him anymore.

When Laura had reached the door to the nursery, she'd disappeared inside without a backward glance, leaving him seething inside. He'd had every right to follow, but suspected he'd reach the doorway just as it was slammed in his face. He could hardly barge inside and glare at Laura or continue their argument with the children as an audience. Mother and Father had done that all the time. His boys were old enough to understand what they said to each other in anger, just as Nash had when watching his parents at each other's throats.

She was impossible, his wife, but damn it all... he had done his best.

He took a deep breath and entered the nursery, surveying the room.

Thomas wasn't at his desk, and Liam was lingering by the window playing with a toy soldier. He fought down his irritation at their lack of attention to their studies.

Yet when the boys saw him, they both rushed to sit at their desks and begin their lessons.

Laura was seated on the floor, on a rug near

an old wooden rocking chair, where she'd put Isabelle down to play with a rag doll.

She glanced at Nash, and then at their eldest son. "Thomas, will you come and show me your work from earlier today?"

"Yes, Mama," he said dutifully, climbing to his feet and walking slowly over to her.

She smiled at the boy, and Nash's heart skipped a beat. Laura's smile had often turned him speechless during the early days of their marriage. When she smiled, the world always seemed a little brighter...but more complicated, because Father would notice and recall him to order, taking him away from her. After a time, Laura smiling at *anyone* had become far less frequent.

She continued to smile softly at their son as he fidgeted before her. She glanced at the book but did not demand to see it immediately. "Tell me what you have there?"

"It's my penmanship book." Thomas held the book closed against his chest. "Miss Sophie wished me to write about the estate, so I wrote about the stables and horses and I drew a picture, too. It's not finished yet."

"I'd love to see it," she promised, and Thomas reluctantly handed over his work.

Laura admired his childish drawing and traced the words he'd scratched out with her finger. The glitter of her gold wedding band on her left hand caught his eye and his breath caught.

"But this is wonderful, Thomas. You've done so well describing everything."

A relieved smile appeared on the boy's lips, and he glanced at Nash nervously before he hurried back to his little desk and bent his head over his papers again.

Nash studied only Laura. When he'd first seen her on the lawn two days ago, she'd been wearing gloves. She had been wearing them when she'd asked for a divorce, too, and earlier this morning as well. But now the gloves were gone, revealing that she hadn't forgotten she was a married woman entirely.

He clasped his hands behind his back, hiding his own bare finger, but very puzzled by her. The first thing he'd done when he'd given up on her and their marriage was to have the too-tight ring cut off his finger.

It was right before he'd attended that masquerade and made love to her, instead of the stranger he'd assumed her to be.

Liam rushed over to Laura next. "Do you want to see my work, too?"

"Of course I do. I want to see everything you want to show me."

Liam did his best to explain his drawing, but it was clear from his description that it was hardly sensible. Still, Laura heaped praise on him, too, ruffled his hair and asked him questions about his life and his favorite animals, which were every animal on the estate.

"I must take you riding one day soon," she suggested.

Liam's eyes lit up. "Do you have other horses?"

Thomas lifted his head from his work suddenly. "Are you going away to take care of them?"

Nash tensed as Laura's expression froze for a moment. But then she laughed softly. "I have one horse, but it is not really mine."

Liam gaped. "Who gave it to you?"

Laura ruffled his hair again. "It's not important."

"Do you have to give it back?"

"Yes, soon."

Thomas scowled. "So, you are leaving us?"

"I don't want to leave you, but..."

Thomas turned his back on his mother. "But you will."

"I missed you all so much," she promised, glancing toward Nash and frowning. "When you're older, you'll come to understand that some things are out of our control."

Thomas shook his head, and he started to write again in his book. But after a moment, he glanced at her. "When Papa goes away, he writes to our governess," he snapped.

Nash winced. "Sometimes my letters have gone astray."

"I'm sure your papa hates being away from you," she said. "But the duke needs him very much. He must miss you both as much as I did."

"More," he told Thomas firmly. "And I came back with presents for you both this time."

Liam spun to face him, full of excitement. "Can I have mine now?"

He glanced at his sons, knowing he had deliberately turned the focus from Laura and her abandonment of their children. The boys were too young to understand the problems of their marriage. It was best they not pester Laura about why she'd gone or would leave again.

Laura lowered her head slightly. "Liam, you should not make demands of your father. He will have to go back to the duke soon."

Nash had hours to spare to be with his children now, and with a wife who didn't want him around.

"I will give them to you later. After supper, perhaps," he said, even as he lowered himself to sit propped up by the wall near the door, one knee raised to lean his arm upon.

He could immediately tell his wife was surprised that he didn't rush the boys away and leave her on her own with Isabelle. She had been very clear about how little she expected from him.

Laura had formed such a low opinion of him over the years, but he smiled knowing that he could prove her wrong today, and perhaps unsettle her, too.

She stared at him for a long time, and then a blush slowly grew on her cheeks. His wife glanced away first, and Nash smiled as her blush continued to color her cheeks.

He had provoked that blush somehow, but he did not know what exactly it had been in response to this time. In the past, that blush had appeared every morning after they'd made love. Was she remembering the happy side of their marriage at last, a side she claimed she did not want from him anymore?

He winced though as Isabelle crawled around the floor near her, exploring her new world and every toy she could put her hands on, which went straight into her mouth the next moment.

Nash had not known Isabelle existed, and he was still struggling to accept that. Her arrival had knocked the wind out of him completely, but he wasn't about to let her out of his sight. He'd little experience with their natures at this age, having left the boys to Laura and the nursemaids to care for them both.

He remained as he was on the floor against the wall, watching the boys attend their studies with a determination that made him so proud, even when Isabelle crawled under the desk and slapped her chubby hands against their legs.

Nash pondered what he could do about Laura and Isabelle. They were going to be living under the same roof for the next month, inhabiting the nursery for all that time. And it was his last chance to speak with Laura honestly before he could never do so again.

Isabelle crawled over to him next, talking to herself in words he could not understand. Her touch on his leg had him looking down into the remarkably pretty eyes of his infant daughter. Eyes that reminded him so much of her beautiful mother.

Isabelle attempted to stand. Her chubby fingers clutched at his knee and her little legs wobbled, and he flung out an arm in case she might fall. But she never did. Her tiny fingers dug into his knee, digging into the fabric of his pantaloons as she wobbled ever closer. Her lips were shining with drool by the time she found her balance, and then she stuffed her hand into her mouth and gurgled.

He smiled at the mess she was making of her smock. "What are you about, my lady?"

Isabelle's response made no sense to him at

all, but she still moved closer. She lifted one foot and put it on him, dangerously near his groin. Fearing she might stomp and cause him pain, he reached for her and lifted her high into the air.

Isabelle giggled and threw all her weight forward.

Nash caught her against his chest. "I've got you, angel."

She made another little cry and wriggled in his arms until her head collided with his cheekbone. Hard. He winced at the pain, but then her mouth connected with his jaw next. He froze, utterly surprised by her baby kiss. Wet, sloppy, and horrible. Yet somehow, adorable. "What a bold girl you are to kiss me like that."

A tiny, damp hand landed against his jaw, and she pinched his face, crying out in the way babes often did when overly excited.

Laura crossed the room and snatched Isabelle away from him. "She's hungry."

"She's teething," he noted.

"Yes, and always eager for what she should not have."

Nash hissed in frustration as Laura took Isabelle as far away as possible from him and fussed over the tiny girl in such a way that meant he couldn't see the child. It was clear Laura adored their daughter, but it seemed she did not want him to do the same. He could have tended the girl if he'd been shown what to do, and he could certainly have given her that dry husk of bread to bite into.

But Laura had always rushed to the children as soon as she thought they would make a fuss, and well before any servant tried to beat her to it.

After she'd left, he'd structured his sons' days to ensure they were never alone or an afterthought. It was his duty as a father to care for them, too.

But Laura had always been more spontaneous than him. She did things on impulse, but that wasn't his way. It was the primary difference between them and the subject of most of their last arguments.

According to Laura, he was too strict, too hidebound and cautious.

If she'd grown up with a father like his, she would have turned out the same. Rules had been the only constant in his life.

But according to Algernon, he had to change.

If he continued to enforce his rules, they would always fight and argue. However, if he let his control lapse for the month, chaos would ensue. The boys would become unruly, argumentative, and not attend to their lessons well enough. Only then might Laura see a schedule was best for everyone. When she finally admitted he was right, he'd be there to step in and take charge.

Laura had never seen the value of giving the children a set of rules to guide their days.

Nash could be as impulsive and unpredictable as anyone. But what was the point in proving her wrong now? She didn't expect him to change. She probably didn't care that he might consider doing so.

He pursed his lips, liking that idea of surprising her, but to what end? They were to divorce. There would be no benefit to him if she liked him better.

He studied her now and shook his head.

The only area of their marriage where Laura had not confused him was in the pleasures they'd shared in their marriage bed. Some of his best moments had occurred in her room, on top of her bed, by moonlight.

No.

She'd made it very clear she did not want him in that way ever again. Time and distance had dimmed the importance of those pleasurable moments for her, it seemed.

But not for him.

Nash had cherished each and every hour they'd spent together at night. He had never truly been comfortable expressing affection where one of his brothers—or his father—might see. Father would have seen it as a sign of weakness.

He hadn't wanted his father or brothers to

suspect how often they were intimate. The younger ones would have teased him about Laura, and that would have humiliated her if she'd overheard it. He'd restrained himself in public for the sake of modesty, too. Laura had been the only lady in a household full of men.

No, for the sake of peace, he would refrain from mentioning again the pleasures she would miss when they divorced. And if she ever remembered and changed her mind, he would let her come to him and beg. Come to *his* room, and there, she would be reminded that he had placed her needs ahead of his own every single time.

He had the night Isabelle was conceived, too.

Even if he had been deep in his cups and too foolish to recognize the beauty under his hands as his very own wife, he had ensured she was sated before he found his own release.

He heaved a heavy sigh of regret and adjusted his position. It had been a long time since he'd sat on the floor like this. It would remain uncomfortable as well, if they only had the one chair or window seat to sit on here.

The nursery was not meant for children *and* both their parents. He would have to make some adjustments to ensure their comfort, too.

And then Algernon expected them to spend an hour a day—as judged by the falling sands of an hourglass—together in conversation with him, explaining why they could never be happily married to each other.

He still did not see the point of becoming reacquainted with his wife, only to give up in the end.

The thought made him sadder than the prospect of divorce had ever seemed before she'd come back.

A scratch sounded on the door before a servant entered. "A message from His Grace."

Nash reached for his note and skimmed it. He was being summoned.

"I have to go," he said slowly, oddly disappointed by that fact.

"Then go," Laura said so dismissively that he felt the barb as a stab through the heart.

"I'll return as soon as I'm free to do so," he promised. "Perhaps we could take luncheon together."

"Yes, please," Thomas and Liam cried out at the same time. Luncheon together often meant a meal taken in the formal dining room, which the boys seemed to love inhabiting.

He had not done that enough with them. It would be his first meal with Laura for several years, too.

He climbed to his feet and glanced at his wife again. She wasn't even watching him, so he rather awkwardly took his leave.

But on the way down the staircase, he could not shake the feeling he was making a mistake. He stopped and glanced up. Perhaps he should have refused the duke and put his family first, the way Laura said she'd always wanted him to. Or they could have come with him.

Nash shook his head and resumed his path to the library, where the duke awaited him. It might be important.

"I appreciate your prompt arrival," Algernon said to Nash as he strode into the library.

Nash tossed the note he'd received into the library fire and threw himself into a high-backed chair. "You summoned me in the same manner Father used to do. A note."

"Well, the discussion of your sudden engagement began in such a manner with a summons from Father," Algernon murmured. "I thought you would appreciate the symmetry."

Nash threw himself into a chair.

"My father did the same to me when Nash came the day after he declared his intentions," Laura added as she entered the room. "You sent for me, Your Grace?"

Nash rose immediately, watching Laura glide into the room toward the duke, a note of summons crumpled in her fist.

"Where are the boys, and Isabelle?" he asked, rather astonished she'd leave the girl anywhere.

"Jasper and Mrs. Radcliffe arrived to take charge of them all," she answered without meeting his gaze, glaring at Algernon. "They were ordered by the duke to take them out to see the horses. I told them they should ask for permission instead, but Jasper ignored my wishes."

The duke shrugged.

"They should be at their lessons," Nash protested.

She met his gaze, defiant. "The minute you left, I let them play."

Nash pressed his lips together, momentarily taken aback by her hostility but not surprised, really. "We will talk about this later."

"You may talk, but I don't have to listen," she said flippantly.

"Now, now," Algernon exclaimed. "Let's not start bickering."

"Too late," Laura quipped as she lowered herself into a chair and carelessly let the crushed note drop to the floor beneath her.

Nash stared at the paper, waiting for her to pick it up. However, it seemed Laura had left the nursery in a belligerent frame of mind, and she would leave the paper there for someone else to pick up.

She noticed his interest in the paper and acknowledged it with a defiant raise of her brow, daring him to say or do something about the mess she'd made.

Nash stretched to pick it up and threw it into the fire as well.

Algernon smiled at them both. "Right. Now. Shall we begin?"

Nash nodded, and Laura did the same.

CHAPTER SEVEN

"NOW, I want to take the two of you back in time to before you were married," Algernon began. "To a time when there was no talk of a marriage between our two families."

Nash frowned. "I thought we were here to discuss our divorce?"

"We will get there in due time," Algernon said and turned to Laura. "Do you remember the first time you were invited to Ravenswood?"

"We came for a dinner, I think." Her brow rose, and then she pointed at the hourglass. "Are you going to turn that thing or must Nash do it for you?"

The duke smiled and turned the hourglass. "The occasion was my eighteenth birthday. Nash was..."

"Seventeen," Laura murmured.

"Laura was sixteen," Nash replied, determined not to be left out of the conversation.

"He had finally shaved off that ridiculous attempt at a beard," Algernon continued, smirking. "He was nervous about his looks, though."

Nash winced, barely remembering himself with whiskers. By all accounts, he *had* looked ridiculous with a feeble amount of hair sprouting all over his face, and he'd been teased to the point of humiliation before he'd had their valet shave it off. "What does my miserable excuse for a beard have to do with anything?"

"Nothing." Algernon turned to look at him. "What did Laura wear to dinner that night, brother?"

Nash frowned, but he easily remembered meeting Laura that night. It wasn't the first time, though. He'd seen her at a distance, and then met her without the benefit of a formal introduction. Their family estates shared a border, and they'd spoken briefly on more than one occasion. Laura had not been out in society yet at that time and he'd not told Algernon anything about it then. "A pink muslin frock with green and gold embroidered vines around the neckline. Laura embroidered it herself."

"Is he right, Laura?"

By his side, Laura shrugged. "He is."

The duke nodded. "And Laura? What do you remember most about Nash that night?"

"He wore a blue suit and silver waistcoat and he seemed..." Laura did not finish her sentence.

Nash leaned toward her a little, keen to know what she had thought of him then. "Seemed?"

"Different," she said, keeping her gaze on the duke.

"Different to what? Had you met before?"

As a blush grew on her cheeks, Nash glanced at Algernon and shook his head, warning him not to press her for an answer.

Algernon nodded but continued to smile at Laura, and the amused gleam in his eye made Nash downright uncomfortable. He and Laura had decided together that they'd not tell anyone about meeting prior to that night.

The duke winked at her. "Right, well...and what was I wearing?"

Laura frowned severely. "Blue?"

Nash shook his head. "Probably black. He wore that color, or lack of, more often than not to get on Father's nerves."

"Wrong on both counts. Never mind." Algernon smiled quickly and looked pointedly at him. "Nash, tell Laura why you dismissed the old nursery maid now."

"Yes, I want to know the reason for that," she

said, turning to him. It was clear it was a touchy subject with her.

"I had noticed her sleeping during the day, napping, when she should have been watching the boys. I assigned another maid to the nursery to observe her for a month, and to help if needed, and she reported back to me that the nursemaid seemed unusually tired for no obvious reason. I took her pulse and found an erratic beat. I ordered bedrest, but she resisted my advice. She passed out on the servants' staircase one day shortly after and bumped her head rather badly in the fall, frightening the children."

Laura's breath hitched.

He continued, "I realized then that her health was in decline, and I sent her home to be with her family with a generous bonus to ensure her comfort for her remaining years. I also spoke with the local physician about my concerns for her and urged him to call upon her as often as possible."

"She never told me she'd been ill," Laura admitted, her posture softening.

"'Tis not an illness but old age," Nash added for clarification. "I hoped that with fewer demands on her time, she would live many long and happy years with her family."

Algernon caught his eye. "Why Mrs. Radcliffe?"

"We met by chance. She needed employment away from London and something instantly available. She was young enough to keep up with the children, and wiser than any young maid here had proved to be. She had experience with orphaned children, and could keep the boys under control and active, too."

Algernon clapped his hands together. "So, the dismissal was a considered decision for the benefit of the old lady's health. Not done out of spite or on a whim."

"Of course not," Nash promised, affronted. "I did what was best for the children."

Algernon turned his gaze on Laura again. "Has he explained his actions concerning the changes in your sons' care while you were away sufficiently, madam?"

Laura nodded, back stiff again and facing the ducal desk rather than Nash. "Yes. I suppose so."

"Good," Algernon said, clapping his hands again and pulling a sheet of parchment out of a drawer. As he ticked something off a list, a pair of servants arrived carrying a tea tray. They set it down behind them and left the room.

"Nash, pour your wife a cup of tea," Algernon ordered.

Nash sputtered. "What about the divorce?"

The duke glared at him. "Do it, or this ends here and now and you can stay married forever. I can easily persuade those with authority to deny a petition from you."

Nash stood, angry with his brother's threat, and stalked to the tea tray. He splashed some tea into a cup, tossed in three lumps of sugar and stirred vigorously. He tapped the spoon precisely three times against the rim of the cup and took the cup and saucer across the room, placing it on the table before his wife. "My lady."

"Don't call me that," Laura hissed. "I'm not your anything."

He scowled and reconsidered how best to address her. He'd never been informal with her in front of his brother. Or any of the family, for that matter. Perhaps he should use her first name, now they were to part ways. "Laura."

"Now, sister dear," the duke said, beaming a smile at them both. "Nash needs a cup, too. Fetch him one, and make sure it's the way he likes it."

Laura scowled but went to the tea trolley as he had done. Nash did not watch his wife but kept his gaze on his older brother. What was Algernon doing, forcing them to make tea for each other?

Laura put a cup before Nash and sat down primly, hands clenched.

Algernon gestured to both steaming cups. "Drink and then describe."

Nash shook his head at the idiocy of his brother's request and took a sip of his tea. "Black tea. No milk or sugar." He set the cup down immediately. "Just the way I like it."

Laura took a sip and then put her cup down more slowly.

Algernon leaned toward her. "Well, sister?"

"Just the way I like it, too," she promised.

"How delightful. You remembered." Algernon smiled widely. "Now, Laura. Would you be so kind as to make a cup of tea for me?"

"Yes, of course. How do you like it?"

"How do I like it? Do you hear that, Nash? Your wife has no idea how the Duke of Ravenswood takes his tea. Nor what a future duke was wearing the first time she came to the palace to dine with us. But she remembers what you, the spare, wore that night and knows your taste in tea without having to be reminded."

"Well, of course she should when she was *my* wife, not yours," Nash complained with a shake of his head.

"Exactly my point. Now go back to the tray and offer a biscuit the other will like," Algernon asked.

There had been two types of biscuits on the tea tray. One Nash liked, a shortbread, and another he did not. He went to the tray and offered

Laura the biscuit he did not like—the one studded with fruit. She set it on the saucer of her tea cup without comment or eating it.

When it was her turn to choose for him, he watched her, curious now. Her hand hovered over his favorite—the shortbread. But then she seemed to consider choosing the one studded with fruit for a long moment. Finally, she sighed before offering him the shortbread. "Your favorite, I believe."

"Thank you," he said, and took a bite.

Laura returned to her chair and stared stonily ahead.

Algernon sat back, grinning at them. "Neither one of you has changed beyond recognition. You remember each other's preferences, and Laura committed nothing about me, the future duke, to her memory."

"Tea and a good memory are hardly important," Nash complained.

Laura huffed and turned her face away. "It's the little things that matter. I always left you the shortbread."

"Yes, Laura, and my point, exactly. Life is made up of a lot of little moments that can easily be forgotten or misplaced through neglect and busyness. The more time you spend together, the more at peace you will feel."

"Peace was never possible when the family continued to meddle and spy upon me," Laura said, scowling again. "Every move I made was reported back to the duke. And nothing has changed here."

The duke pursed his lips. "Laura is correct. The duke spied on us constantly. He was always complaining about her. The servants were reporting her every move to him."

Nash felt her eyes upon him, but he did not turn. "Algernon, you will not spy on Laura or use the servants to gather information about her activities like father did. She is my wife still, and I won't have it."

Algernon nodded. "Beyond these meetings of ours, I promise not to interfere. I shall stay well back and let you both have the run of the place with only one rule—you may not sleep on different floors of the palace again. You will continue the occupation of adjoining bedchambers. No more sleeping in your study, Nash."

Nash reluctantly nodded. "Agreed."

Laura said nothing.

"Well, time's up. I won't see you at dinner since you'll be with your children. Do have a pleasant evening. Your children should be in the nursery again and a pair of horses have been saddled by now. I asked Jasper to go down to the stables to have them made ready and waiting for you to both ride the estate together after our hour."

"So much for you not interfering," Laura cried, irritation obvious as she burst to her feet. "I've no desire to go riding, so I'll be in the nursery with my children."

Laura shot out of the room before the matter of riding could be discussed further.

Nash bowed his head. Algernon could not help but meddle.

"The horses do need the exercise," Algernon explained with a careless shrug. "She used to enjoy riding the estate with you. But, if you two will not take the horses out, I will have to ride one and lead the other, or conscript a stable hand into coming with me."

"I could still come with you?" Nash offered. "I could use the fresh air. The palace can become stifling, especially when stuck with someone who doesn't want me around."

"Then you realize how Laura must have felt when you were gone from the estate." Algernon shook his head. "No. You must stay with her and tend your responsibilities. I won't become our father and demand all of your time."

"You couldn't even if you wanted to," Nash assured him.

Algernon grunted. "You're flattering the

wrong person. Go after your wife and children. They need you more."

Nash grimaced but nodded. The meeting with Laura had done no good at all other than prove how impossible the situation was. "Laura doesn't trust us."

"She has good reason not to. Father manipulated you both into thinking the worst of each other. No wonder she left you, and you left her."

"I did not leave my wife," Nash promised.

"Didn't you?" Algernon tipped his head to one side, studying Nash. "I hardly ever saw you in the same room together after the first year of marriage, except for formal dinners. How could you bear to leave her alone here for so long?"

"You know why I had to." He'd done it for Algernon and their brothers. Nash rose to his feet and studied his brother, sitting at their father's old desk. "You won't learn how to make a good marriage from our example. What are you trying to achieve by dragging up the past?"

"I'm trying to help you find common ground so you can hold civil conversations around the children. If I can make you both as happy as possible from those discussions, then that will be for the good of all, too," Algernon explained, throwing up his hands. "Surely you don't want to stay angry with each other?"

Nash shook his head. "I don't think it's possible to be happy without a divorce."

Algernon stood and came around the desk and settled a hand on his shoulder. "I know this is difficult, but trust me, talking about the past is essential. You'll get there in the end if you both stop fighting each other. Excuse me."

"Where are you headed?"

"To take those horses out. Maybe Jasper will come with me."

He left the room, and Nash followed. He probably should seek his other brother and talk to him about Sophie. He'd been taken by surprise by their announcement, and he did not want to be at odds with Jasper. He would congratulate them on their upcoming marriage and wish them well.

The duke suddenly staggered backward, holding out one arm to stop Nash from continuing down the hall with him.

He pivoted on his heel and pushed Nash back, hard. "We can't go this way."

"Why not?"

Algernon laughed softly, leading him back the way they'd come. He leaned close. "Love matches are always the worst. Couples make love at the drop of a hat when they think there's no one around to disapprove of their fun."

Nash glanced down the hall, astonished by

the idea that Jasper and Sophie might be... "Now?"

"Now," Algernon insisted. "We'd better get that pair wed by special license as soon as possible, I suspect."

Nash shook his head. Sophie had always seemed so proper to him, despite the circumstances he'd found her in when they'd first met. She'd lost a child and hadn't had the benefit of a marriage. She'd been betrayed and tossed aside like garbage. Through all of that, she'd kept her dignity and had never once given him a sign of interest in other men. Of course, now she was to marry his brother, he did not think less of her for being swept away again. Jasper would marry her. "Yes, it might be a good idea to expedite that marriage."

"Agreed," Algernon said as he rubbed his hands together. "I suspect there will be so many babies filling up the nursery soon that we will have to expand it."

"Yours should be there already," Nash chided.

"I never said I didn't want children," Algernon promised. "Or if I did, it was always within Father's hearing, which, let's face it, was everywhere. I've said a great deal of nonsense over the years just to get under his skin."

"You enjoyed it," Nash said with a half laugh,

stepping out of doors and into the sun. A stable hand stood not far away, holding two horses. "I could come with you. On horseback, I mean."

Algernon seemed to consider his offer, then shook his head. "No. Better not resume bad habits. You have a wife and a family. I would send you home to them if we did not share the same house."

"This *is* my home," Nash protested.

"I never said it wasn't," Algernon promised. "But as we get older, there will often be times when we are too busy for each other. When I marry, I will be with my wife and children more often than not, I expect."

"Unless you're with Lady Barnes," Nash suggested, glancing at Algernon in curiosity. "You keep a mistress. A wife would not be happy about that."

Algernon smiled quickly. "I will not keep a mistress when I marry. I had already stepped back from my connection with Lady Barnes when Father died."

"You never told me," Nash said, shocked that the affair was over. "What happened?"

Algernon's jaw clenched for a moment, and then he shook his head. "I cannot marry Lydia or have legitimate children by her. And I certainly don't wish for Lord Barnes' demise. So, I have begun my fresh start, just like you."

"I'm sorry. I know you were very fond of her," Nash murmured, recognizing sadness in Algernon's eyes and voice.

"I will always admire her," Algernon admitted. "And I shall forever regret what could never be."

Lydia, Lady Barnes, and Algernon had been close for many years, and yet they could never be together. Algernon now had to marry a woman he might never learn to love.

His brother slapped him on the shoulder and pushed him away. "Think not of my loss, but of your gain. How do you want to live here in the years to come? Will you at least try to make yourself happy?"

"I want to," Nash promised. "I will be content, I suppose."

"That is less than I wish for you and for our brothers," Algernon promised. "You must have love and happiness, whatever it takes."

Algernon threw himself onto a horse and took the stable hand with him. Nash let him go, but his heart was heavy. He did not know what the future held in store for anyone, but more complications seemed likely in *his* future.

Laura would go, and Isabelle would stay. Sophie would marry his brother Jasper and the duke would finally wed one day. Stratford had already gone off with his bride and wasn't expected to return to the estate for some time.

Nash was a loose end. The odd one out again. Unhappy being married, but unable to do anything about it still.

That wasn't what he'd expected or hoped for by his age. He was filled with the same uncertainty now as when he'd proposed to Laura and became a husband.

CHAPTER EIGHT

LAURA ANSWERED the next summons from the duke at her own pace. Slowly. She'd been putting Isabelle down for her nap when a maid had arrived with the news the duke wanted to see her again.

Only this time, the maid informed her she was to escort Laura all the way there.

But she could not go yet. She'd been trying to get Isabelle to sleep for the last hour. She had asked Nash to take the boys outside to play because they were such a distraction for the little girl. Nash had been reluctant to leave them, but he'd finally left Laura to it. Laura had almost succeeded until the maid's knock. Now she needed more time to send Isabelle off to sleep. The duke would just have to wait.

"Good morning," Jasper whispered as he

slipped into the room, his hair standing up, his clothing in disarray.

Laura groaned under her breath but continued to rub her daughter's back, hoping Isabelle did not sense her irritation with yet another interruption. Her daughter clearly heard Jasper but at least she did not sit up to look at him.

After a moment, Laura glanced at the windows where rain beat against the panes. "What are you doing here?"

"The duke sent me up to see if I could help."

"So much for the duke not interfering," she murmured. "I don't need help. She needs silence."

"Of course she does. So I'll sit with her while you're away."

"Aren't there more interesting things for you to do?"

"I enjoy watching the rain from these windows," Jasper promised. "It was the only time Ravenswood felt cozy when I was a boy, up here with all my brothers."

"Nothing can make Ravenswood feel as cozy as my childhood home was," she insisted, keeping the motion of her hand on Isabelle's back constant.

Jasper drew closer and leaned over Isabelle's cot. "Well, not everyone was lucky to have parents who showed them they were loved. Mine were distant figures. I barely remember Mama. I was fonder of the cook, to be honest."

"I'm not surprised," she replied and held her breath as Isabelle's eyes finally closed. "But I am sorry you were not loved as a boy."

"I had Algernon and Nash to love me, and my little brother. But I could bear one of these of my own," Jasper whispered, leaning out to lift Laura's hand away from her daughter's back and taking over with the rubbing at the same speed. "I've got her now. I need the practice," he said, and then winked.

Laura straightened up, suppressing a groan as her back protested. She'd been bent over that cot for too long, determined she didn't need any help. She watched Jasper for a moment and realized she couldn't do everything for her children. Jasper really was the most affectionate of the brothers, and it showed in how he cared for his niece. "How did you know Nash loved you?"

"He was always there, watching over us. Even from a distance, when he wasn't around, he'd enlist trusted servants to follow us about. Keep us out of trouble and Father's way, too. A gardener for the outdoors, and a footman for inside, for instance. You had them, too."

"Spies," Laura muttered, cross about that still.

"Well, if Father had his, Nash had his own,"

Jasper murmured, as if there was nothing wrong with that. "It's no different from those with two parents. One parent is always strict, the other lenient. Or so I hear."

"There is a world of difference," Laura protested.

"Not if the result is the same. We were always taken care of by Nash and Algernon. Always fed, dressed appropriately, put to bed. Educated. Nash was a rather excellent teacher, although he nearly had to sit on me to keep me at my desk sometimes. I much preferred going outside than reading all day long."

"As do I," Laura told him. "I used to ride every day until..."

"Father gave your horse away," Jasper murmured. "It was his, not ours. Nothing could have stopped him doing as he pleased with his property."

"He considered my children his property, too," she complained.

"We all were," Jasper agreed. "You were the lucky one. You got away."

"You could have gone, too."

"I could not have abandoned my brothers to deal with him alone," Jasper said. "We swore an oath to protect each other."

Laura scowled at him. "But not me."

"We did what we could," he said, then glanced at the door. "He's waiting for you."

Laura turned. Nash was there, silent, listening and the boys were with him, restrained from coming in by his hands on their shoulders. They moved back, making room for her to join them in the hall. She slipped out of the nursery with the maid following and shut the door quietly.

"I am summoned," she told Nash.

"You all are," the maid told them. "If you could all follow me downstairs."

Laura exchanged a glance with Nash, but he seemed just as puzzled that the boys were coming with them. She didn't really want to ask Nash about it in front of them right now. She was tired and longed to rest.

At the stairs, Nash slipped his hand under her elbow again to steady her down the first flight of steep steps. For the next, he let her manage alone.

The maid turned them in the opposite direction of the duke's study today. She led them to the ballroom doors and flung them open. Laura had not been in this room in years, and it seemed to have lost some of its grandeur and sparkle. But perhaps that was only because it was still daytime and she was weary.

Aside from attending balls, which had been

rare, she'd never been permitted in here with the children.

The boys ran inside to the duke, where he stood at a window looking out on his domain. Nash's hand slipped under her elbow again to propel her across the threshold and toward him.

The maid quickly shut the doors behind her, leaving them alone with the duke.

Ravenswood turned and smiled, hourglass clutched in his hand at chest level. "Thank you for coming," he called.

"It's not as if he gave us any choice," she muttered to Nash.

"Let's hear him out before we start bickering," Nash suggested. "Brother, what are we doing here?"

"It's time for a little instruction," he said, setting the hourglass down on top of a pianoforte.

Laura stopped, and Nash did, too. "Instruction in what?"

"Dancing. The boys are overdue for lessons. I thought I could help you help them."

"We don't need help or a ballroom for dance lessons," Nash said. "We taught ourselves in the nursery and hallways."

"However, the pianoforte is here, so the lessons will be held here, too. How else can they see the grace they must strive for unless they have the right example to follow and the music to dance to? Humor me."

Laura sighed heavily. She was not in the mood to dance, but she could play for the boys. "Very well."

She started toward the pianoforte, but Ravenswood shook his head and placed his hand on the instrument. "I will play, you and Nash instruct."

"You don't play the pianoforte," Nash argued. "You've no musical talent whatsoever."

"Don't I?"

Ravenswood sat down at the instrument and played a lively little piece very well. He played it so well, in fact, that Laura was impressed.

Nash sputtered and uttered an oath. "When did you ever learn?"

"Lady Barnes taught me," the duke admitted somewhat sheepishly. "Father never knew. You know how little Father thought of men with accomplishments he thought belonged only to women."

"You were lucky he never found out," Nash answered, drawing closer to watch his older brother.

The duke hit a wrong note and winced. "Unfortunately, I play better when no one is watching me too closely."

Nash immediately turned his back and stared

at Laura. After a moment, he nodded, and stepped toward her. "That's the song we danced to that night you first came here."

Laura remembered the night too well. "It was played a little faster, I think."

"I play at the speed I can manage or I make many more mistakes," Ravenswood warned them. "Boys, come stand by me while your parents dance together. Watch them closely now."

He paused his playing and turned the hourglass so the sand began to fall.

"What's that for?" Liam asked him.

"It's to keep track of the time your parents spend together," the duke answered. "Don't touch it, or I'll get in trouble."

Laura narrowed her eyes on the duke, but suddenly Nash moved between them again and his wide chest was all she saw. He approached her, his hands outstretched. "Might I have the honor of a dance, Lady Sweet?"

"As if I have a choice," she muttered darkly.

"The children are watching and listening," he warned quietly. "We're supposed to prepare them for when they join polite society."

Defeated by that argument, she curtsied, murmured her agreement to dance and put her hand in Nash's. The duke played, and they danced together. It was odd, being the only couple twirling about in the large room. Especially odd when she hadn't expected to be in Nash's arms ever again. Determined to get through the dance without a misstep, she kept her gaze past Nash's shoulder as they spun around the room.

Her boys were watching them, Liam leaning against the pianoforte, suffering no punishment for his untidiness, but Thomas was watching them with his arms crossed. He reminded her of Nash in that pose. So unwilling to bend or smile.

"You dance beautifully," Nash murmured. "As graceful as I remember."

"Your memory is faulty, my lord. I stepped on your toes the first night we danced. I am woefully out of practice," she warned.

"But so am I," Nash assured her with a laugh. "In fact, I have only ever danced with you."

She glanced up at him. "Was there no one at the masquerade to tempt you to dance?"

"Only you. But my mind was interested in another form of dancing. So was yours, I believe," he suggested.

Laura gulped. "A temporary aberration brought on by too much wine."

"You don't drink wine. You only drink water," Nash said, and then stopped. He bowed to her. "You were the only one with a clear head that night." He turned away and called out, "Thomas, come dance with your mother."

Liam rushed over, though. "What about me?"

"You are next, lad," Ravenswood promised him. "Come sit up here next to me on the stool. We'll play together."

Liam rushed to his uncle. "Can I really?"

"I don't see why you cannot learn." The duke shuffled along the seat and devoted his attention to Liam, who banged on the keys without any skill at all.

The duke laughed and started to play when Liam finally stopped.

Laura smiled at Thomas, encouraging him closer, but Nash took charge, turning what should have been fun into a serious lesson. He ordered him to hold her hand and she could tell he didn't want to. Nash took a place behind Thomas. "I'll direct."

"Of course you will," Laura muttered.

They began. Badly. Thomas had some idea, but his stride was shorter than hers and *much* shorter than his father's. He kept stretching his legs too far and stumbling because of it. His face slowly reddened with embarrassment as Nash corrected him repeatedly.

After a while, Laura wet her lips and suggested a change. "Perhaps Thomas and I should try this alone."

Nash considered her request and immediately stepped back. "Very well."

"Right. Now..." She glanced down at her son and smiled. "Thomas, the man must lead on the dance floor, so I am completely in your control. You decide where we go and when we change direction. I will follow you everywhere."

Thomas nodded, his face so very serious as they began to dance again. Laura moved with light, tiny steps, and they did far better together than they had before.

Nash prowled the edges of the room, watching them closely with a hawklike intensity. His scrutiny was unsettling for her, and she thought for Thomas, too, when he noticed his father watching.

"You're doing well," she whispered to her son.

"I want to be as good as Pa is. He never stumbled."

"You will be with practice. He was not born a dancer. No one is good at anything on the first try."

That seemed to reassure Thomas, and his shoulders relaxed a little. He was almost smiling when the duke suddenly stopped playing to growl, "Liam, what did I tell you?"

"I was just looking at it," Liam promised and quickly scurried away from the duke. He ran to Laura and hid behind her skirts.

Nash rushed over to the duke. "What happened?"

The duke held the hourglass out and shook it. "Didn't you see?"

"No, I was watching the dancers."

"Liam grabbed the hourglass while I was playing and turned it over a few times. I've no idea which way was the right way round now."

As Nash turned away from his brother, Laura caught a ghost of a smile cross the duke's face. Ravenswood quickly schooled his features again and looked cross, but she'd seen enough. The duke had somehow manipulated Liam into turning the dashed thing for him—probably by telling him not to.

And that meant there was no way to know when their time was up anymore. She raised a brow at Nash to see if he realized they were being manipulated, but he only shrugged.

"Continue."

Liam tugged on her gown. "Will I still get ice cream?"

She scowled at Ravenswood. "Bribery now?"

"Everyone likes ice cream," he answered with a careless shrug.

"Not everyone," Nash tossed out. "My wife does not, for one."

Laura turned to Liam and cupped his face.

"I'm sure the duke will deliver it to you personally today, too."

Liam's eyes widened with excitement. "Uncle Allan always gives us the biggest bowls."

"Uncle *Allan*?"

The duke grinned. "A little informality never hurts at his age," he suggested, sitting down at the instrument again.

"Of course." Laura marched across the room and snatched up the hourglass. She took it to the fireplace mantelpiece and set it up high, where Liam could not possibly reach it again.

She turned and smiled sweetly at the duke. "There. Now there can be no more ill-advised turnings to prolong our meetings."

"It was just a bit of harmless fun," Ravenswood complained with a laugh as he played again.

Liam tugged on her skirts again. "Is it my turn to dance with you now?"

She glanced at Thomas, but he'd retreated to stand with his father during her exchange with the duke. "Why not," she said and began a different dance with him.

Dancing with Liam, who was a foot shorter than his brother, involved more awkward turnings and stomping on toes, but much laughter.

Nash was covering his mouth by the time Laura stumbled to a halt. Utterly exhausted and over her anger at the duke's manipulation. She had enjoyed dancing once, but had done little of it lately.

"My turn with Mama again," Nash announced.

Before she was prepared for it, Laura was hauled into Nash's arms and twirled rapidly around the room. She barely kept up with him and eventually begged for him to slow down before she fell. He did so slowly, pulling her closer to his chest as the duke played a strange tune. Something beautiful and rather romantic, in fact.

Laura glanced up and became caught in Nash's gaze. They danced, and the room, their children and even the music faded away. There was only the two of them, holding fast to each other as they moved as one.

But she was again in danger of becoming enthralled to a husband who would only hurt her. It wasn't fair.

She stiffened, and Nash brought them to a halt though he didn't release her immediately. His fingers slid across her upper back, onto her bare skin. His other fingers caressed the wedding band that still rested on her ring finger. He pressed, holding it tight, and his head slowly lowered toward hers. She inhaled the scent of him just before his lips brushed hers.

She stumbled back from him, panicked by his attempt at seduction.

"Laura, wait—"

"No. Not again," she protested, looking around the room. But there was no one with them anymore. They were alone. "Where has the duke taken them?"

He followed her. "For ice cream. What is wrong?"

She looked at him with annoyance. "You know exactly what is wrong! The duke has taken my children."

"No. They left with the duke as soon as we started dancing, to get them the ice cream you agreed they could have. In fact, you ordered the duke not to disappoint Liam."

"But I heard music playing," she said, stunned that she'd not noticed them all go.

"Laura, there was only the music of our hearts guiding our steps when we danced."

She gaped at Nash. The last thing she'd ever expected to hear was him spouting a line that could have been romantic had it come from anyone else.

He shuffled his feet. "We were always perfectly in tune with each other when we danced... and when we were alone in your bed."

She gulped, unfortunately remembering everything about those intimate moments with

Nash far too clearly for comfort. "Perhaps it would be best to wait until you have hired a new governess and dance instructor for the boys before you continue the lessons. After I'm gone. Excuse me."

Nash, however, wouldn't be left behind. He followed her, claiming he wished for iced cream, too. Except she remembered Nash had never cared for sweets before either. It was something else they had in common. In fact, he had given the cook a lecture once about how damaging such a treat could be for the boys' teeth.

At the stairs down to the kitchen, he grasped her elbow again, and in the narrower flight, she couldn't escape the fact that she appreciated his help. But what she did *not* appreciate was the fact that her body still wanted him close. And sometimes, so did her foolish, traitorous heart.

CHAPTER NINE

ALGERNON SWEET WAS as transparent as glass. Laura knew what he was attempting to do with these ridiculous hourglass meetings between herself and Nash. She'd suffered two weeks of embarrassment as they rehashed the past, but the hours always ended the same way. Her leaving flustered and Nash irritated.

It seemed Nash saw little wrong in the way they had lived together as man and wife before the old duke's death, or if he did he didn't admit it before his brother.

Algernon, though, clearly believed that they had too much in common, remembered too much about each other, to ever let their marriage end. He was relentless, dragging out the smallest, most insignificant spats and moments as if they had been earth-shattering events. What they were, collectively, was a sign of how wrong they'd been together.

Unfortunately, discussing those memories hurt and exposed wounds she'd thought were long healed. Yes, she knew how Nash took his tea, and what he was wearing the night they first danced together here, and how handsome he'd looked that evening.

He had been asked to partner her, and she'd spent her first nerve-racking dance in public in his strong arms.

Later, he'd done his duty again and proposed marriage to her, instead of Algernon being forced to do so.

Yet, like many other arranged marriages it was done to provide the one powerful family with the dowry from another ambitious family. Father had wanted the distinction, and any match to a brother would do for him after Algernon refused to offer for her. Laura had done her duty and agreed because, out of the two brothers, she had preferred Nash's company best of all then.

He was bright and well-mannered and she could find no fault in him then. But his consideration had been an illusion because he had ceased caring about her opinion as soon as their first son was safely delivered.

When the marriage was dissolved, she would

have autonomy for the first time in her life, but she would have to relinquish control over her children to their father permanently. She'd never had any say in how they'd ever been raised until now and after the divorce her influence would be fleeting at best.

The future without Nash was full of uncertainties. Still, it was a heady feeling to know a complete escape was almost within her grasp.

If only they could talk about the future and not constantly revisit the past. She would like to make arrangements to visit with her children upon their divorce. To have something concrete written down and beyond dispute or discussion.

But the duke was determined to discuss and pick over every facet of their failed married life first.

The hourglass on the corner of his desk seemed to take an eternity to empty some days. "Now, Laura. I want to discuss Isabelle. Why did you not tell your husband you carried his child before Isabelle was born?"

Laura inhaled. "I didn't want her taken from me."

"I would not have done that," Nash insisted.

"But you would have insisted on dragging me back here for the birth."

"So I could take care of you," he said, not looking at her.

She sighed. "That is why I couldn't bear it again."

Ravenswood frowned. "Is there something wrong with a husband taking care of his wife at such a time?"

"All he cared about was seeing another heir for the estate born healthy," she insisted.

"That is not true. I cared about your welfare, too," Nash replied.

She turned to stare at him. "And after? Besides knowing to the day when we could share intimacy again, somehow, I hardly saw you once Thomas and Liam were born. After months of coddling, suddenly you were never around."

"I left a nursemaid and father had his physician here," Nash reminded her.

"Yes, and he visited me too often," she said, shuddering. "Your father believed the cure for my bouts of melancholy was to have me bled."

Nash exhaled. "No. I gave strict instructions you were not to be."

Laura narrowed her eyes on him. "Do you really believe your father agreed with that? I tried to tell you. I wrote."

"I received no letters from you."

They stared at each other a long painful moment and Laura saw the exact moment Nash realized he had been manipulated.

She faced the duke, unsettled by his shock.

The duke's expression though was dark, furious.

She inhaled a shuddering breath. They really hadn't known. "After Liam was born, when Nash and everyone was gone from the estate, I was doctored almost to death's door at your father's order. I could not help but cry somedays and your father had no compassion for women. He insisted I be bled to calm my nerves before I saw the children. Eventually I became too weak to climb the stairs. I could barely rouse myself out of bed most mornings and I feared then that my husband would not come back. I had no choice but to leave and save myself. It was the only way I could have survived."

"I didn't know," Nash whispered in horror. "I swear I did not know about any of that."

"I wrote to you about it," she said, brushing her left arm, her worst scar lay hidden under the long sleeves of her gown. She could never uncover her arms in public again. People would whisper about the damage done to her skin. "I gather your father read my letters and disposed of them."

"Why did you not tell me or anyone of us what was going on," Algernon asked softly.

"His grace made sure I was never left alone with any of you for long enough once his special treatments started," she noted. "And there was always one of *his* personal servants hovering nearby whenever I had strength to leave my room. They would call you away if our conversations continued beyond pleasantries."

Nash drew close. "I received no letters, no warnings of what was going on here, Laura. I thought you angry with me for being away again and never wrote."

She sucked in a sharp breath. "I was angry with you. I am still angry."

Nash bowed his head. "And given what I've heard today I deserved that anger. I did not protect you and I should have."

An uncomfortable silence descended upon them and Laura let out a shaky breath. There. The worst of it was out in the open.

Algernon slammed his palm the table. "I remember Mother being bled, especially after Stratford was born. No doubt that's where father got the ridiculous idea it was beneficial for a ladies health."

"And a fine way to control a disobedient woman with no husband around to notice," Laura whispered.

"I told him again and again that its madness to bleed too often," Nash growled. "He could have killed her."

"I think that was the intention, brother," Algernon murmured with a shake of his head.

"Damn him, a thousand times over," Nash cursed, bursting to his feet. He stormed about the room, raking a hand through his hair.

Laura smoothed her skirts over her thighs. Her cuts had long since healed but her fear was still there. "When Isabelle came I was relieved she was born a girl. The Sweets never seemed to have any interest in their daughters until they neared marriageable age. She was safer with me and I thought you would only have been disappointed that I delivered a daughter anyway."

"That is not true," he swore, returning to his chair and pulling it closer to hers.

She let out a shaky breath, struggling to contain her emotions. "I was nothing in this family but breeding stock."

"She has a point," Algernon said, surprising her with his agreement. "Father treated Mother poorly and tried to force you do the same to Laura, as well."

"I did not treat Laura as breeding stock." He insisted. "She was my wife."

"Yes." She dropped her eyes. "And you couldn't wait to get back into my bed after Liam was born too."

Nash hissed. "Because I enjoyed being with you! I liked..."

When he didn't continue, she glanced at him.

He was staring at Algernon, head tipped to one side, an odd look on his face.

"Very well," the duke said and stuck his fingers in his ears. "I won't listen. Continue."

Nash leaned toward her and his hand landed on her arm. "I enjoyed watching you climax."

She stared at that hand on her arm, troubled by how quickly the warmth seeped through her sleeve. His hand covered some of her worst scars that had been gouged too deeply and the slowest to heal. She flicked his hand away. "How could you see me? We always made love in complete darkness."

"There was often moonlight, but perhaps saying I watched you is the wrong term." Nash glanced at his brother, then leaned closer still to whisper, "I could always tell when your peak approached. You would twist and writhe. Grab my hair, my body, and then sob my name. My eagerness to return to your bed was to satisfy my need to satisfy *you* again."

Laura met his gaze and instantly felt a surge of desire rock through her entire body. She blushed, remembering all too well how it had felt to have Nash near in her bed at night.

Yes, Nash had been an exciting visitor to her bed. She had not believed it was for her benefit as much as his, though.

But given the look in his eye, the words he

said now, she grudgingly accepted he might mean it.

She gulped, unsure of what to say to him now. He had never once left her unsatisfied. He was watching her now, waiting to hear that she had enjoyed his attentions. But if she admitted how much she had, she feared it would weaken her argument for their divorce.

She glanced at the duke sitting nearby with his fingers in his ears and his eyes turned to the window to give them some privacy, and then the hated hourglass between them, just as the last grains fell.

"Time's up," she whispered.

Laura stood and walked calmly from the room despite her husband's entreaties to stay. She slipped into another chamber and leaned against the door as her legs buckled. She sank untidily to the floor, ashamed and embarrassed.

The trouble with her marriage was that the intimacy between them in bed at night had been unforgettable. Always pleasurable, but when dawn came there was only ever emptiness that remained and a dented pillow where his head had been.

She couldn't go back to that wretched existence. Waiting for him in vain.

A knock sounded on the door. "Laura," Nash whispered.

Damn him.

Could he not give her a moment of peace? She shut her eyes and willed him to go away, but of course, he knocked again. "I wanted to visit your family's estate and make sure all is well there. If you want to come with me, I can have your horse saddled and made ready for you. I'll wait for you at the stables for one hour."

His footsteps went away, and she put her head in her hands. She wanted to go home desperately, but she did not have one anymore.

She took a deep breath and climbed to her feet, feeling steadier.

Home had never been Ravenswood, but an estate now irreparably changed by the fire that had consumed it.

However, it was curious that Nash suddenly wished to view the ruin where she'd hidden herself for a few days after all he'd heard today. That estate was none of his concern. He could not inherit it through their marriage and nor would she.

She went upstairs to her children but was informed the duke had conscripted Jasper and Sophie to watch over them for a few hours more.

"We have no objection," Jasper promised, jiggling Isabelle in his arms and tickling Liam. "I've grown quite fond of playing with them all."

They were the picture of a happy family. Without her.

She ground her teeth and considered ordering them out, but she *had* left something of hers in the ruins of the estate and wanted to fetch it back herself. "Careful, Jasper, or you might end up with a dozen of your own."

"If they are as adorable as these three, then I would be a very lucky man indeed," he promised, and then kissed Sophie's cheek.

Laura winced, hating the feeling of jealousy that rose at the obvious affection between the newly engaged pair. It was a reminder of what her own courtship and marriage had lacked.

Eventually, she nodded. She trusted Jasper and she would have no opportunity to return until after her thirty days here were up.

Time was short. There were two weeks left of their arrangement and she couldn't seem to go anywhere without her husband following two steps behind lately.

A maid was waiting in her room to change her into a riding habit on the duke's order. It was an old gown of hers. Something she'd left behind when she'd fled her marriage and forgotten all about. "Where did this come from?"

"It's from your other trunks. The ones Lord Nash ordered stored, and then had brought down from the attics not long after you returned. My apologies for taking so long to air and press everything ready to wear again."

"Show me," she said, curiosity getting the better of her.

She went to the adjoining dressing closet and instead of the few gowns she'd traveled with, she found a mountain of garments she'd almost forgotten, including the ballgown she'd worn when Nash had proposed. Of course, it did not fit her anymore.

The collection was everything she'd left behind...and more that she could not remember purchasing. She sorted through everything, puzzled by the unexpected excess. "These are not all mine."

"Oh, but they are," the maid promised. "I remember when the last delivery came. You were gone from the estate. But they were all hung up in wait for your return but...but you never did." The maid winced. "They stayed untouched until last year, when Lord Nash ordered everything packed away."

Her breath caught. Had Nash purchased her new gowns while he'd been away from her? She hadn't been here to receive them, of course, but Nash had not known that at the time. And he'd kept them hanging in her wardrobe until a year ago.

A year ago, she had been carrying his child and more determined never to come back to him.

Just when she thought Nash was truly heartless and cold, she finds out he'd done something nice for her for a change. It was too little too late, of course. A few pretty dresses and sentimentality hardly made up for the emptiness he'd left in his wake.

She changed into the older riding gown, glad it still fitted her, and asked for all the garments with short sleeves that would reveal her scars to be packed away. She made her way down to the stables when that was done.

Nash was looking out over the grounds, changed already. One booted foot resting on the ladies' mounting block as he looked over his family domain. He was not the young man she'd married and yet he was the same in many ways. Handsome and always so wretchedly serious.

He turned before she reached him, and his eyes swept over her from head to toe. But he did not smile and said nothing as he helped her mount her horse sidesaddle.

He swept up onto his own horse and led the way from Ravenswood without a word. Once they had left the estate behind, he brought his horse into step with hers. "I wanted to talk to you out here about what happened while I was gone."

"It's in the past," she said, shrugging.

"But it isn't, is it?" He sighed. "You bear the scars to remind you every day of my failings. You were right to leave, to protect yourself from further harm. My only regret is that I cannot turn back the clock and do what needed to be done."

"What was needed?"

"I should have killed him for the pain he caused you," Nash said and then kicked his horse to a gallop.

Laura did not follow him but she watched him ride away, clearly angry and not wanting her to see his fury. Laura had not that need anymore. She had cursed the old man, and Nash, too, until her throat was hoarse. Now all she felt was emptiness where hope should have been.

Eventually Nash returned, windswept but appearing somewhat more composed. He apologized for riding off so suddenly and she forgave him. They crossed the border and left Ravenswood land.

"The place is badly overgrown, I fear," Nash warned, ducking as low-hanging branches began to impede their way. Finally, the crumbling outbuildings came into sight. "Perhaps we'd best travel the rest of the way on foot."

"The path is perfectly safe for riding," Laura told him, taking the lead. She knew her way home like the back of her hand. She was no stranger to the ruined estate. She had come here several times since leaving Nash, not that he seemed aware of her visits to the district. The first time was to put flowers on her parents' graves.

Her home had once been so beautiful. Warm and inviting and a place filled with laughter and love. But now it was only an empty, burnt-out husk. Full of scorched timbers and fallen masonry. Any laughter long gone.

Laura had already left Nash when the manor house had been lost. The fire seemed to have started in the observatory. All the glass was gone, melted into puddles and mixed with ash. Likely a candle had been left lit and caused another spark that, unnoticed, had let the fire spread until it was an unstoppable blaze.

She had lost her father in that blaze. Her mother had already passed away before she'd been brought out. Her brother had suffered minor burns to his hands, or so she'd heard.

But the extent of the damage had been so great that the estate was abandoned almost immediately by him, and he began a thoroughly disreputable life at his other property south of London where he'd died.

Laura turned her horse toward the kitchen garden and followed the enclosing wall before dismounting, using the mounting block.

"Well, here it is in all its glory," she murmured. "Home."

"Ravenswood is home," Nash countered.

"Never *my* home," she reminded him. Walking on to get a better view of the building and away from her husband, she could feel the sadness and dread this old place inspired returning to depress her spirits, just as bad as it had the first time she'd seen it all.

Her old room on an upper floor was long gone, all that remained in a livable condition was a small portion of the servants' quarters, the part half buried into the hillside beneath their feet.

She headed for the only working doorway.

"Are you sure it is safe to go in there," Nash called.

"Safe enough for me," she answered. "Remain outside if you are afraid."

"I am not afraid, but I would not like you to be hurt."

"You never worried about me these past years," she replied.

He rushed her and caught her arm, held her back. "I worried about you, but what could I do when you left no forwarding address?"

"You did not look very hard. I was found within a month," she said, glaring at him. "Offered a safe place to stay away from the rest of the family."

"Who took you in?"

"Does it matter?"

"Yes, it matters because you *didn't* stay away from me," he hissed. "You came back to me once. You seduced me."

"Seducing you was a mistake I will not make again," she promised.

He pursed his lips. "Is Isabelle a mistake to you, too?"

She ripped her arm from his grip, annoyed that he would use their daughter as a weapon to hurt her. "I could never regret Isabelle. She is my daughter. My blood. My family. What I regret is my own weakness. The wife you knew is gone, Nash. Just like the fortune I brought to our marriage, I assume. That is the only reason for the duke to keep me here, hoping I will comply with his wishes. The funds I brought to our marriage swallowed up by the needs of yet another duke."

He held her in place. "What have you heard about that and from whom?"

She had but one source of reliable gossip about her husband, and she would not betray them for the world. Not after all they'd done for her. "The old duke was fond of spending money he simply didn't have, and lived on credit. And you had *my* money and gave it to Algernon, didn't you? I'm certain you've paid whatever debts Algernon inherited from the old man to save face until he takes a rich wife."

"We *all* have offered whatever money we have," Nash admitted, which surprised her. Once they'd married and he had her dowry, she'd been constantly informed that matters of money and finance were none of her concern. "We had hoped Algernon would be quick about making his choice known."

"Quick is not Algernon's way. He is very much like your father. Waiting and watching for the right moment."

"Algernon has many responsibilities and problems to attend to first. Whoever he marries affects us all."

"Not me. Not anymore, though I suppose our children will always suffer his whims, since he's almost as fond of ordering our lives as your father always did. You don't wish to be with me."

"I wished to go riding with you today," Nash insisted.

"But was it your first thought or his suggestion? Have you ever just put your foot down and said no to your family?"

Nash suddenly stomped said foot.

Laura stared at her husband, startled.

He winced. "Spider."

She glanced down to see the large flattened creature revealed when Nash lifted his foot. Laura yelped and scurried back from her husband. Nash stooped to pick it up with a stick and immediately carried it away from her.

Laura removed her gloves and wiped her damp hands on her riding habit.

He came back quickly, dusting off his hands.

"It won't bother you again." He smiled quickly. "I still remember how much you dislike them."

She exhaled a breath. "Jasper always thought my fear highly amusing."

"Jasper learned the hard way that teasing you was not something to do again," Nash promised.

"The hard way?"

"A dozen such creatures left in his bed one night ensured he was no longer amused by spiders and developed a fear of his own."

She glanced at her husband in surprise. "You did that to one of your brothers?"

He nodded. "I would not let them torment my wife as they might try with me."

"Yet your father could not be stopped?"

Nash continued down the abandoned hall. "Obviously not. He was the duke but if he was here now there's no telling what I'd do to him."

She hurried after him down the dark passageway, surefooted in the gloom. "Did you hate him?"

"I..." Nash shook his head. "I feared him. He was my father. I wanted to please him."

"And did you?"

"In some things, I suppose I came close," Nash admitted as they entered the kitchens. It was cold and dank, barely discernible with the feeble light leeching through high, grubby windows. He looked around, prowled the room, inspecting everything that remained. "The room is fairly dry. I had believed the house was damaged beyond repair down to the foundations."

"My brother probably wished it had been so," Laura suggested. "He was much happier in London."

"You were with him there?"

"No. I was staying with a friend of mine."

His gaze narrowed. "The year when Isabelle was conceived."

"Obviously, that year."

Nash nodded. Unnerved by the calm way he accepted her words now, Laura turned away from Nash and went to a cupboard. Inside was small statue she'd found forgotten in the rubble. While her back was turned she whipped off her wedding band from her finger too and clenched it in her fist for a moment.

She would not take the ring with her when she left, though perhaps Nash would give it to his next bride. Her fingers clenched the ring even tighter and she forced herself to drop it on the shelf and closed the door.

Laura pulled on her gloves quickly to hide her bare finger as she realized her husband was standing directly behind her back again.

He cleared his throat. "Why?"

"Why what?"

"After all that was done to you, why approach me in London? Why risk being found? Father was still alive then."

"I wanted to see if you remembered me."

"I never forgot you. But that woman reminded me of you so strongly, I broke my vows with her."

Laura sighed. "She was me."

"I wanted her to be you, too, and I made myself believe it didn't matter that she wasn't."

She waited for him to say more, but he did not utter a word. All she heard was his breath, fast and close by. She shivered, remembering all the times they'd met in the dark of her bedchamber. "We should head back to Ravenswood," she whispered.

"Not yet."

"I want to see my children."

His fingers settled on her waist. "I want to see you."

She swayed toward him.

"I want to see the scars."

His words were like a bucket of water tossed over her head. "But I don't want you to."

Laura turned and strode out of the old kitchen, pretending she wasn't terrified of her husband's disgust when he saw her arms, and left Nash to find his own way out.

She was mounted on her horse, and impatient to be on her way, by the time Nash finally emerged. He was frowning and looking back at the ruins of her former home. Assessing the place, she assumed. "The kitchens are sound," he said. "It's a pity the rest may never be rebuilt."

Laura marveled at the way Nash could switch off the intimate parts of his personality in an instant. "Yes, it's a great pity. The expense of the repair would bankrupt anyone who thought to try."

"Most likely. Still, a will and beneficiary is being looked for."

"I wish them luck."

He mounted his horse and drew near again. "Would you not want to see it come back to life one day and have a family live here again?"

She did, but she couldn't bear the thought of it, too. She would never come back here again. It was too painful. "No," she said, turning her horse away from the ruined manor house and Nash.

She dashed away the tears falling down her cheeks with the back of her hand before he saw them, vowing it was the last time she would cry over the past.

CHAPTER TEN

NASH STROLLED BACK to the palace from the stables, following Laura at a distance, troubled by her last words when she'd left him by the ruins of her family estate. She'd galloped away on horseback, but he'd known there were tears shed.

Laura had been tortured here.

There was no chance she would ever forgive him for that, nor should she.

He had hoped she might come to appreciate the vast opulence of his family estate the way he still did, but that was before he knew the truth about what had gone on while he was away the last time. The memories she had of his home were not happy ones.

How could they be.

It was much too late to make any difference now. Nothing he said could make it right again. So much of their marriage had been spent apart.

He'd seen their estrangement happening but hadn't known how to make things any better. Father's demanding ways had been a source of tension between them from the start.

So had his need to be a dutiful son and protective brother. He'd sacrificed much to protect his siblings, and that had continued in the years of their marriage. He'd sought peace in the family, but he had not achieved that for his own wife.

And attempting to appease Father hadn't stopped the man from trying to ruin the estate Algernon was to inherit, either. Nash had worked hard to temper the worst of his poor decisions, running around behind the scenes to make sure things got done without Father knowing.

He'd thought the bulk of Father's venom had landed on Algernon. But Nash had come in for his share of disdain, too. Only the existence of his sons, the next generation, had given him any respect in his father's eyes.

But to learn now what had been done to Laura while he was gone, what had driven her to abandon their children and him, made Nash's blood boil still though he was trying not to show it.

If only Father had left Laura alone, they might have stood a chance of becoming what Laura had hoped for. What he'd hoped for, too.

"I say, Lord Nash, you look like you're ready to murder someone?"

He pivoted and saw a distant neighbor, Lord Guildford, on the lawn, with Algernon standing silent at his side and smiled. "Hardly, I'll join you later."

Nash continued on into the house and up to his bedchamber, intending to change out of his riding clothes but he didn't know what to do with himself after that. He was not really in the mood for the company of a nosy neighbor, nor the duke either.

His mind continued to spin.

Every bleeding held the risk of death. For Laura to believe her life in danger meant the bloodletting had been very bad indeed. She was not given to flights of fancy. If she'd believed herself in danger, then she absolutely had been.

And where had he been? Running all over the countryside while his wife was unprotected.

It was his fault. The separation, her anger. Isabelle.

All of it.

Nash collapsed into a chair and put his head in his hands.

He could never make it up to her. They would never find peace together.

Their marriage was over, but until today he'd

not realized that he had still harbored a secret hope it could be saved.

He looked up and his eyes fell on the sketch of Laura hanging on the wall beside the door connecting his room to hers. She hadn't changed a bit from when he'd drawn her, and yet he was seeing her with a clearer vision than ever before.

She could hardly stand to be here given what had been done to her. It was only the children that kept her here.

Nash snarled at the closed door and went there to open it. Laura was not inside her room, but it was obvious she had been. Her riding gown was spread across a chair.

He stepped farther into the room and inhaled deeply. The room smelled of her perfume and her. A dozen of her possessions, powders and creams, were scattered over the dressing table surface.

He touched nothing but drank in the scent of Laura's perfume, and let out a shaky breath. Despite her belief otherwise, Laura had always belonged at Ravenswood. It should have been her home and a place of safety. She should never have been driven to leave it.

Nash would allow no one to interfere in her life ever again.

Only he and Laura should decide the course

of their lives from now on, and he vowed they would suffer no more interference from anyone.

He left through Laura's room and stepped out into the hall. He headed for the stairs and looked up. The nursery was one steep flight of stairs above their rooms, and he couldn't hear his children or her. He'd never been able to. He had always disliked the distance, but Father would never hear of them having chambers closer to his own and Laura's.

But there were many empty rooms at Ravenswood.

Rooms that used to be occupied by elderly relatives, long since passed and closed up. There was even an empty apartment, comprising a quartet of bedchambers and a large sitting room, on a lower floor. It wasn't directly accessible from the main part of the house and thus never used anymore.

Curious about the state of those rooms, he headed downstairs but found the doors stuck fast. He put his shoulder into it and the doors burst open. A cloud of dust rose around him and he sneezed.

When the dust settled, though, he looked about and saw what he expected. Dust cloths covered everything and the curtains at the windows were half rotting away in their places.

However, the apartment had definite possibilities for him and his family.

He walked around slowly to avoid disturbing more dust and looked into every nook and cranny. Yes, definite possibilities. For him, three children and even...for a *wife*.

He closed his eyes. Laura would not be staying.

Feeling frustrated again, he stalked to the window and tried to look out. The pane was so dirty he had to rub a spot clean with his thumb.

The duke and their neighbor Guildford were walking together upon the lawn directly beneath them. But Laura was with them now, talking to the newcomer.

Suddenly he remembered: Guildford had studied medicine in his youth.

Nash nearly tripped over his own feet in his haste to return downstairs and protect his wife. It was irrational, but the fellow always asked after her health.

As he drew closer, he noticed an expression of concern on Guildford's face as he spoke with Laura.

Nash's unease grew. He joined them, placing himself near his wife so there was no doubt who she belonged to.

"Ah, there you are, brother. I was afraid you had forgotten us."

"What are you doing here, Guildford?"

The duke coughed.

"Well, I chanced upon the news that your lady had returned to Ravenswood. I had to come and see for myself that it was true and pay my respects, of course. It is a pleasure to have her back among us and looking so well, isn't it? The last time I saw her she was terribly pale."

Laura said nothing but continued to stare at the man.

Nash shifted closer to his wife, setting his hand under her elbow. Ready to support her if need be.

Guildford laughed wagged a finger at him. "Still as devoted to your wife as ever, I see. I completely understand, and I'd be the same if I were married to her. She is lovelier than ever. After so long apart, I wouldn't want her out of my reach, either."

"Nor will she ever be again," Nash replied, ruffled by the suggestion that she would be soon.

Laura moved toward Guildford, slipping from his grip in the process. "Shall we go inside and take tea?"

"Only if you will accept my escort," Guildford answered, smirking at Nash. "I should love nothing more than to spend an hour in your company, my dear."

When Laura accepted his escort inside, Nash

could only grind his teeth impotently. That should have been *him* escorting his wife inside, now she'd finally come home.

Algernon grabbed his arm when he would have followed. "I need to speak with you before we go in."

"We spoke earlier," he answered, trying to follow Laura and Guildford.

Algernon, however, would not be stopped or allow him freedom to go after her. "I just remembered something I'd forgotten. It could be helpful."

"Very well, but only for a moment," Nash agreed.

Algernon headed for his study and Nash followed along. The duke shut the doors. "What do you remember of the party the evening before your wedding day?"

"Impatience for it to be over. Why?"

"Do you remember if Guildford attended?"

Nash frowned. "He did not, that I recall."

"When Guildford arrived today and smiled so warmly at Laura, I remembered something that I had forgotten all about." Nash could feel an icy hand settle between his shoulder blades at the long, drawn-out pause. "Guildford held a *tèndre* for your wife before your marriage, didn't he?"

"I don't remember that," Nash said, inching toward the study doors. He was more worried about Laura being alone with Guildford due to his medical training than any foolish romantic notions Algernon might harbor.

"Of course you wouldn't remember. You only saw Laura once you became engaged, and it's not as if Guildford would say anything after the engagement was announced."

"Then why do you mention it now?"

"It's not what he did then, but how he looked at her today," Ravenswood said quietly. "He disappeared as soon as the engagement was announced, avoided us all for months after the wedding as well...but after each child was born, he comes to call on Laura. He's not here to see me or you. He came for Laura."

Nash's blood ran cold. "There's nothing between them."

"Not today, but who knows what tomorrow will bring," Algernon said, grinning. "Think about it. This is almost too perfect a solution. You and Laura still want to divorce. So if she marries Guildford, the children will still be able to have their mother visit them as often as she likes. Perhaps they could even stay with her on Guildford's estate when you're away or have a second family to tend."

"I would *never* let my children live anywhere but Ravenswood."

"Well, that is for you to decide in the end, of

course. Laura will have no say and must abide by your wishes about that. But I won't stop her from visiting them here. And if Guildford doesn't suit her for a second husband, there are other bachelors of a suitable age in the district that I'd image might fancy her for a wife."

Nash bristled. "It is not up to you to suggest anyone for her to remarry!"

Algernon spread his hands wide. "But brother, what can it hurt to nudge things along in that direction? It would be best to broach the subject with her before she decides where she'll go to live."

The duke continued, unaware that Nash was wishing he could strangle his own brother to shut him up. Guildford could bleed her again and no one would be able to stop him.

"Look, you can discuss the matter with Laura during our meetings, or I am offering to mention it instead. Get the suggestion out in the open. It's not as if you seem to want her still and she doesn't want to be here after everything done to her. I could even offer to host her wedding breakfast, if that would help speed things along and reassure her of our support."

A fine film of rage washed over Nash as he imagined a wedding breakfast held here, with Laura kissing some other groom. He fought jealousy, fisting his hands by his sides rather than following his instincts to shut the duke's mouth with them. "You will say nothing to her about this ridiculous idea of yours!"

"But Nash, where did you imagine she'd go? She can't stay at those ruins of her old family home. She has to belong somewhere."

"She belongs *here*." He shook his head stubbornly. He could not tolerate Laura living in squalor. It was bad enough she'd spent even one night there alone. "I will talk to her about her plans for the future later."

The duke smiled brightly. "All right, then. I'm glad you're keeping an open mind and want the best for her. I know I was against the divorce, but after seeing you two bicker constantly over every little thing these past weeks, I concede I might have been wrong that your marriage could be saved. Now, we'd better go join your wife and her potential beau and act as chaperones, so there is no hint of impropriety. We wouldn't want any scandal surrounding Laura's second marriage, now would we?"

Algernon left the room first, but when he went to follow, Nash's legs refused to work properly. He staggered toward the bookcase to hold himself up as his stomach churned. He'd never bothered to imagine Laura's life after the divorce in detail, other than the disgrace that might follow them about for years. He'd only thought about what *he* wanted.

But of course, there was the very real possibility of her being married again. She would need a home, protection. That Laura could marry someone he knew bothered him a great deal.

She might even come to love them.

His stomach flipped alarmingly.

Laura, his beautiful wife, could belong to someone else soon. She would take their hand, pull them into her bed and give her body, her limitless passion, to them alone in the dark.

A privilege he'd taken for granted.

He cursed under his breath.

Of *course* Laura would eventually marry someone after they divorced. She would need the company and protection of a man who did a better job than he had.

Nash would never want her to be all alone.

But she *would* be alone unless she remarried.

And right now, Laura was in the drawing room to take tea with a potential suitor who might doctor her to death one day. And although the duke was joining them, Nash was uncertain he could be trusted. Not when he was so keen to have Laura married off almost immediately after the divorce was final.

Nash hastened to join them, but he pulled

himself to a stop outside the drawing room doors, just out of sight of the occupants to listen. He heard the duke and Guildford speaking, but Laura was oddly silent. Was she enthralled by Guildford's conversation? Was she sitting there wishing she'd married him instead, now, too?

Well, she had not. Laura had married him and was still his lady. *His* wife.

He smoothed his hair, straightened his waist-coat, and, after a moment's hesitation, strolled in as if he owned the room.

Guildford smiled his way, but he barely cared about the man's welcome. Nash searched the room for Laura.

But Laura was not in the room anymore.

He glanced at the duke and raised one brow.

Algernon smiled. "She just went looking for you. As you can see, Guildford, my brother and his wife can barely stand to be separated. Never satisfied unless they know exactly where the other is these days."

"Even after so many years apart?" Guildford asked, and his gaze landed on Nash's left hand, where his ring ought to be. "Where was she all that time, I wonder?"

"I have always known my wife's location," he bluffed. "We wrote to each other often," he continued, ignoring how Algernon gaped and then quickly hid the expression.

Guildford seemed to consider him overlong and then shrugged. "I'm surprised you would even let her out of your sight after what I heard of her illness. I never would have let her leave Ravenswood. She was terribly unwell I heard. But now that I've seen for myself that my fears were unfounded, I must take my leave and spread the word. I trust you'll convey my apologies to your wife and my profound regret for being unable to stay longer. But I will return to speak with her on another day."

"Of course," the duke said. "You are always welcome."

Nash could not find words that would convey his satisfaction at having the man leave so soon and merely nodded.

He watched the man go in silence, observed the duke begin to grin as soon as Guildford was out the door and on his horse again. "He admires her still, I'd say."

"You will say nothing about that man to my wife, or I will never speak to you again."

The duke sauntered closer. "Does the thought of a rival irritate? Your wife is lovely and young enough to bear another man his heir. Guildford does need an heir. I'm sure he'd waste no time bedding her."

Nash lashed out, striking the duke squarely

on the jaw and sending him reeling into a chair that shattered beneath him.

The duke lay stunned a long moment among the debris, and then he smiled again. "Fight it all you want, but this divorce is the last thing you really want, isn't it?"

"You're wrong," he insisted.

"Can you imagine her lying in a strange man's bed, waiting for Guildford, wearing only a smile?"

Nash took a step toward the duke, fists rising. Yet his greatest fear was Laura weak after being bled again and that he wouldn't be there to stop it. "Get up and say that again!"

The duke wisely stayed where he was. "Be angry with me if you like, brother, but it's yourself you should be furious with. She was your match, and you let her slip through your fingers. Shame on you."

Before he could react, he heard a gasp behind him. He knew who it was without turning.

Laura rushed to crouch beside Algernon. "What is going on?"

Nash glared at Algernon who wisely held his tongue.

"I tripped and fell," Algernon told her.

"Where is Guildford?"

"Gone but he'll be back soon I expect," Algernon promised her and Nash gritted his teeth at the certainty of that.

Since Nash could not hit his brother again, nor admit what had really provoked his anger enough to make a fool of himself in front of his wife, he barreled from the room as fast as his legs could carry him.

CHAPTER ELEVEN

LAURA STEPPED BACK from the duke and watched her husband rush away. "What happened?"

The duke chuckled. "Nash lost his temper. The chair suffered for my impertinence."

She frowned. "Nash doesn't have a temper."

"Oh, yes, he does when it comes to you. It was something that should have come out a long time ago, too," the duke said as he rolled to his feet. "Guildford has left in case you were interested."

"Good," she said, utterly relieved. Laura had dawdled in her search for Nash to avoid speaking to Guildford again.

The man had offered to be her personal physician after she had married Nash and had renewed his ambition again today. It had taken all her strength to hold her tongue about the chances of that happening.

She did not trust anyone with just enough medical knowledge to boast about it. They were a danger to everyone. Nash knew enough to tend minor wounds incurred on the estate. But he always deferred to an experienced hand if he could. Guildford had spent barely a year learning the craft and thought that more than enough to advise everyone he met, too. She wished he'd stop calling on her at Ravenswood to enquire after her health.

She studied the duke and noticed him rubbing his jaw. "Are you hurt?"

"Not exactly," he said, and slowly straightened his cravat.

"Where did Nash go?"

She would like to avoid him. She was out of sorts still, and Guildford's concerned sighs had made her feel anxious again.

Laura huffed as she noticed Algernon smirking, now. She added him to the list of irritants in the day. "The one thing I disliked intensely about you was that I never could get a straight answer out of you."

The duke laughed. "I'm sure Nash has gone upstairs. After all he heard today I'm sure the children will calm him. Perhaps you'll feel better if you join him there."

The children had that effect on her, and she *would* go to them soon, except that Algernon was not above employing manipulation to get what he wanted. He always wanted her and Nash together in the same room. Although he usually never did his brothers a disservice, to *her*, he had become an obstacle in her path to freedom. Ravenswood was not convinced that a divorce was necessary, but it was.

"I'll take a walk in the garden instead."

The duke nodded. "I'll come with you. In fact, I insist upon it."

She could not refuse the duke. But he was likely scheming again and eventually she would find out what it was. She would wait him out and not ask. As long as he did not lead her directly to the nursery, she would play along for now.

The duke led her outside, away from the paths she usually took. They walked in silence for quite some time. Laura refused to be the first to start any conversation with him.

Eventually Algernon sighed heavily. "I see you are still as reluctant to amuse me as you ever were."

"If His Grace requires entertainment, he has three brothers, an estate full of servants, or he could hire a companion to laugh at his jests."

The duke barked a laugh. "That's what I always liked about you. You are as direct as Nash, and with no care for the result, too. I will tell you one truth each day."

Now that was too much to resist. "Did your father leave you heavily in debt?"

"Yes. Horrible of him, wasn't it, but typical and expected. Did Nash tell you about the money situation and his loan?"

"Not in so many words," she admitted.

"With luck, his plan for economies will work and all my brothers will be repaid in full within two years. Three at the most."

Laura's stomach clenched. No wonder the duke was opposed to the divorce. He had to pay compensation to her for a failed marriage. Father had done at least that much to protect her. "So a Duke of Ravenswood actually intends to repay his debts for once?"

"I am not my father," Ravenswood promised. "I did not like the way he treated you, either. But..."

"But what?"

He squinted into the sun. "I was not your husband, Laura. Had I interfered, my father would have assuredly used my interest in your well-being to drive a wedge between us all."

"He did that anyway."

"Yes, and no."

She let out a sigh and stopped. Algernon was not to blame for her marriage. His father had been, but Nash was culpable. Algernon's only fault was keeping her here for these thirty days before he gave his brother his blessing. "You could marry an heiress and pay them back immediately."

"Would you of all people really want me to marry in haste after all you've been through?"

She considered the duke a long moment and imagined the sort of bride he would have to choose to repay his debts. "Perhaps not."

"Believe me, I do not want to marry in desperation for a large dowry, but I may have no choice."

Was he saying his brother had done that with *her*? Laura cast her eyes about the grounds, looking for an escape from the only plausible conclusion she could reach. There had been an obvious urgency to set a wedding date between her and Nash. She had believed Nash eager for their union.

Algernon touched her hand, drawing her attention back to him. "When you left us, I must admit I was upset."

"Why? No one wanted me here."

"Yes, that is somewhat true, but not for the reasons you imagine. Like everyone else, I wanted you away from our father, or him from you. I did not like the way he spoke of you to my brother, and I did not like how Nash ignored it. Had I known how bad it was I swear I would have taken you away myself."

"Nash was ever your father's puppet."

"Reluctantly. For the whole of our lives, we have done all we can to protect each other." The duke pursed his lips. "Did Nash ever tell you that, for a time, Father doubted Stratford was his son?"

"No," Laura admitted, shocked by the suggestion.

"Threatened to send Stratford away, claiming he was weak and therefore no child of his. Father said he had proof that might have upheld a claim of adultery as well. There was admittedly a brief friendship between our mother and another man around the time of Stratford's conception. Father threatened to humiliate Mama and disinherit Stratford right until the day she died. He spoke of it to Nash and me often."

"I did not know that," she answered.

"But it was foolishness, of course. Stratford was obviously cast from the same mold as the rest of us were. To prevent him from disowning our baby brother, Nash rashly made a bargain with Father. A promise that had consequences for your marriage, unfortunately. When you left, Nash was forbidden to follow you, or he'd risk Stratford's place in the succession, and besmirch mother's reputation in the bargain. He adored Mama."

"And he loves his brothers more than anyone," she said, and then stopped. "Why are you telling me this now?"

"When did I ever have a chance to talk honestly with anyone?" he asked with an arched brow. "You know firsthand how cruel my father could be. Twisting the truth until it fit his purpose. Anything Stratford and Jasper did wrong as children, Nash and I accepted the blame for. Nash took many of the punishments meant for our young brothers' supposed disobedience as if they were his own failures, and mine as well, sometimes."

Her breath caught. "I wasn't aware of any harm done to him."

"Not on his skin. Father was too smart to cause physical harm to us. He needed healthy sons to torment, and to give him heirs when I refused to marry and sire mine at his command. Nash learned early to hide his feelings, lest they be used against him. I think he did it too well. When I refused to consider the notion of a match with you, Father took what he thought was his revenge, permitting Nash to marry you, and thereby threatening my place in the succession when your sons arrived."

"I see," she answered, dismayed that Nash

had been manipulated into choosing her for his wife.

"No, I don't think you really do. Nash wasn't unhappy about marrying you at all."

Laura shook her head. "He did his duty to his family."

"It was not duty when he married you. Nash was glad. Glad for me to remain a bachelor. But glad mostly for himself. It is the only truly selfish thing he has ever done in his life."

She frowned.

"It has never been easy to tell when Nash liked anyone, especially women," the duke said, one brow raised. "The danger of revealing any interest was too much of a risk for him. Father inevitably used such instances to wring further obedience out of us all. That's probably why Nash never mentioned his earlier conversations with you. Those times your paths crossed on the estate before you were formally introduced and brought out. They were his secret."

"But you knew," she accused.

"He was too anxious the night of that first ball you attended. Painfully nervous about his appearance. He was first downstairs to greet all the guests, complained at me for being tardy, which he never does. And then you were there, and he blushed," Algernon said, laughing softly.

Then his brows drew together in a deep

frown. "When we were young, Nash had a favorite dog. Clever thing. Obedient, smart enough to learn tricks. The animal was exceptional. Nash adored it. When Father saw the bond between Nash and the dog, he said the dog was *his* property. When Nash protested, Father shot the dog right in front of him. Nash was punished for crying. Solitude for a month in the nursery, although we all visited him each day in secret. Then not long after that, Mama died, and we could not mourn *her*, either. Nash learned never to show how he felt about anyone beyond his brothers after that—especially you."

"I always knew the duke was cruel," she whispered.

"Is it any wonder Nash pretended not to care about you?"

"He did it so well I still believe it," she said bitterly.

"Think for a moment. If Nash was cold to you, it was likely so Father did not realize what you meant to him."

"I meant nothing." She took a step back from Algernon. Algernon knew his brother better than anyone. Better than she certainly did or ever could. The duke believed he was telling her the truth as he saw it. "Your father is dead and nothing has changed here," she began.

"The habits of a lifetime are hard to break.

Even now when I enter the ducal study, I tense up, expecting to face my father again and be given a set down. It took me months to sit behind that enormous desk without jumping out of the chair every time someone knocked on the door. Our father left an impression, a mark, on each of us. Stratford perhaps is the most fortunate. We made sure he was spared the worst of it."

"You will do and say anything for your brothers," she said sadly.

"We will do anything for our *family*, which has always included you. Give us a chance to prove we are not your enemy. The enemy was Father, and each of us must shake off the chains he bound us in, in our own way. Especially Nash."

"What have you done to free yourself from his memory?"

"I was intimate with a woman on my father's desk before he was even buried in the ground."

Despite the scandalous nature of the confession, Laura couldn't help but laugh. "He would have been outraged."

The duke's grin was vicious. "I do hope he died a second time."

"And Nash? What has he done?"

The smile disappeared. "Nash remains bound to the past in many ways still. He needs help."

"And you won't help him?"

"I always help him, but he needs more than me. He needs your help and understanding. He needs your forgiveness now, too." The duke frowned. "You were beautiful, charming, and bright. You had a fortune in a dowry that any man would covet. You would have made an extraordinary duchess. Mother would have approved of you taking her place, had she lived long enough to see the day come. Did you never wonder exactly why I didn't want you for my bride when I could find no fault with you?"

"You told me you did not care for a marriage arranged by our fathers," she replied. She remembered feeling relief that he would never ask. "I was glad, too."

"Yes, I noticed you were not heartbroken to be denied the title of duchess," the duke said, and smiled again. "I much preferred you as a potential sister. You are the only woman who can make my brother happy."

At that, he turned away abruptly, leaving her standing in the garden with his last words ringing in her ears.

Had she ever made Nash happy? Certainly she'd tried, but she had only really succeeded in the bedchamber. Outside of it, she'd failed. He'd wanted nothing to do with her outside of the bedroom.

Was all his coldness and indifference really caused by his father?

He'd been constantly under her feet since she'd come back, yet he seemed much the same. The duke had ordered them to spend time with each other, so Nash was not spending time with her by choice.

She heard a step and spun about to find Nash not far away.

He blinked, as if taken by surprise by her presence in the garden. Then he scowled. "I thought you would be with the children."

"The duke said *you* were with them." She looked Nash up and down, surprised by his rumpled state. His cravat was hanging loose, his hair was a mess. He looked...unhappy.

"I'm not, obviously." He shuffled his feet. "Are you on your way back to them now?"

Normally she would have answered yes, if it meant she could get away from Nash. Today, after all the duke had said about his childhood, she became curious about all the things her husband had never told her. "I was going to walk the grounds alone, but your brother insisted on coming with me."

Nash glanced around the gardens, eyes narrowed. "Where is my brother now? What did he say to you?"

Why did Nash look so worried? Did he not

want her to know about his struggles? "He talked of nothing important. I don't know where he's gone now, though. He just left."

Nash glanced down to his feet, and then his gaze rose slowly to meet hers.

A flush of heat bloomed over her skin at the intent look in his eyes. She wet her lips and his gaze became fixed on her mouth. Her nether regions quivered with remembered anticipation of what his mouth could do to her body. She turned away fast, disturbed by how quickly he affected her. "Join me for a walk if you wish, or don't."

She began walking, and suddenly Nash was at her side.

"Did you enjoy Guildford's visit?" he asked.

"It is always pleasant to meet one's neighbors."

"Only pleasant?"

She winced. "Guildford talks of old times with a great fondness that I don't share. The duke joined us and ordered me to go find you."

"I was in the study, where the duke had left me. He knew exactly where I was the whole time."

"Well, he did not deign to tell me that," she said sourly. "Can a Duke of Ravenswood ever not scheme and manipulate?"

"Probably not," Nash admitted. Suddenly,

Nash gripped her bare hand. "Where is your wedding ring?"

"I took it off."

"When?"

"Today," she said, chin rising. "It's not as if you wear yours anymore."

He slipped a hand under her elbow again and turned her about. "Come with me."

"Why?"

"Because I want to talk to you alone."

He marched her toward the orange grove, which seemed deserted at this hour. Laura tried to subtly shake him off, but Nash's grip only tightened more, though it was not painful.

The edge of the orchard was the place where they'd first met, well before they'd been introduced. Laura had snuck onto the estate on a dare from her brother to pinch an orange for her supper. Nash had found her, though, and instead of being angry and giving any cry of alarm, he'd taken one from the tree himself and peeled it with a pocket knife before offering it to her.

He had been very sweet and kind and promised that she could return whenever she liked. They'd met there several more times, until all the fruit had been harvested.

It had been the perfect place for them to talk, private and far from his family and hers. A place where she'd begun to care about him. They had not come here together even once after their marriage though.

She glanced up at Nash now, and there was such a look of grim determination on his face that she was worried. "What is it?"

"Wait," he demanded, and then he guided her to sit on a bench seat the workers used.

He did not sit beside her today, but began to pace back and forth. She waited, deciding that whatever he was preparing to say must be difficult for him.

He turned to her abruptly. "Why did you agree to marry me?"

CHAPTER TWELVE

"YOU ASKED," she answered immediately.

But Laura was clearly surprised by his question. Her eyelashes fluttered, and then she looked away from him. Her brow furrowed, and when she looked back at him, her gaze became full of sadness. "My family expected me to marry well, but I...I did not want to become a duchess."

He fell back a step. He'd never known exactly why she'd chosen him and it bothered him not to have realized that before now. "You could have chosen any other bachelor in the district, Guildford, for example, and not become a duchess. Why me?"

"We were not strangers, Nash." She sighed. "For as long as I can remember, my father talked of the importance of an alliance with your family. I was told that I must attract Algernon, and for a time I thought I could stomach such a cold-hearted pursuit to make my father proud. But it soon became apparent that we had nothing in common. He certainly had no interest in me. At least, not romantically." She wet her lips. "And he told me so, before anyone else found out his actual feelings about taking a wife."

Nash stared at her, at the blush lingering on her cheeks and the way she fidgeted with her ringless finger. "Algernon told you he didn't want you."

"Yes, we met by chance here, and I thought he was you at first so I called out your given name as I had begun to do."

"Algernon does nothing by chance," Nash mused, rubbing his jaw. "He was attempting to play matchmaker even then."

"Yes, I realized that much later." She sighed. "After a few pointed questions about our secret meetings, he laid out his plan to thwart his father, and mine, as well about avoiding a match to me. He said that no matter what happened, he would always admire me but never propose. He said I ought to ...well...consider another. I appreciated his candor but I was worried for my future prospects. A match between us had been long talked of for so long and you know the harm that spiteful gossip can do to a young lady's reputation when an expected proposal never comes."

"But why me?"

"You were always kind to me. I liked you and you liked me." She sighed. "I admit I also hoped that marrying you would quell any gossip and appease my father. To have any connection to your family was always his goal. Algernon had repeated his threat not to marry anyone at all by the time you asked."

"So you turned to a contingency plan of marrying the spare instead." Bitterness welled inside him and he turned away. "We marry and our children would someday inherit. There was still a possibility that you'd become a duchess should anything happen to my brother."

Laura laughed softly. "There was never any chance I would become a duchess, or that our children would inherit Ravenswood. Algernon *will* marry, but only when he's good and ready. Though I pity the woman he picks."

His spine straightened. "What is wrong with marrying my brother?"

"Please," she chided. "Algernon is as devious and manipulative as your father ever was, though not cruel. He is always meddling and he started so long ago its second nature now. I have barely got a straight answer out of him since the day I married you. His wife will need to have the wits and intelligence to keep up with his schemes, and lots of money too. But, given his propensity for matchmaking his siblings, it's clear your brother is a firm believer in love matches, which is why he's not married yet. He's still looking for her."

Nash considered that rather bold assessment of his older brother. Father had been a cunning old devil, and Algernon had taken on several of his bad habits to survive. He was not always completely truthful. Father had been livid that Nash had asked for Laura's hand without asking for his blessing first. Nash had known he'd never have gotten it. But he'd asked her and then sealed their engagement with a public kiss at the ball that very night.

Algernon had acted as surprised as anyone and was slow in congratulating them. But was it an act? Had he wanted Nash to marry Laura and removed any impediments that might have gotten in Nash's way? It seemed that way now. He spun back to find Laura standing behind him. "Is he really that much of a romantic?"

"Oh, yes," Laura promised with another soft laugh.

"He's met and bedded many women," Nash mused out loud, deciding for honesty—no matter how distasteful Laura might find his words.

"I've heard the rumors, but there's been none he cannot live without," she replied. "Not even Lady Barnes. Don't look so surprised that I know he keeps a mistress. Your father did not lower his voice when he raged about your brother's affairs and his failure to do his duty."

She had a point that he might be. "I think he loved Lady Barnes," he admitted.

"Perhaps he did, but he cannot marry a woman already wed," Laura said with a shake of her head.

Nash shook his head. "I believe you had other options than me for marriage. You will in the future, too."

She sighed. "I don't have any ambition to marry a second time."

"Why not?"

"That part of my life is over." Laura shrugged and placed her hand on his upper arm. "Nash, you gave me three children I adore and want to see as often as you will allow me to. I know they must live here with you, or wherever you go. A second family would demand all my time and loyalty."

He looked down at her hand on his sleeve, astonished that she would deny herself the security she deserved from a husband. "Is it because I was so bad at it?"

"No," she admitted. "I just don't wish for more than I already have."

Her touch continued, light and maddeningly soft on his sleeve. Laura clearly still had the power to set all his senses alight. He did not dare mention the touch for fear she would pull away from him yet again. Outside of the bedchamber, they had touched so rarely. Had she any idea what it did to him now?

Yet, the need to touch her, too, outweighed his caution.

Slowly he moved his hand toward hers, where it rested on his sleeve, and covered it with his palm.

When she startled, attempting to pull her fingers away, he caught them, and they became entwined. "It hurts to think of you all alone, waiting for the next time you can see the children again."

"It is a small sacrifice for those I love," she assured him.

A profound silence fell over them, punctuated only by the sound of her breathing. He shifted toward Laura, and she looked up into his eyes again. Hers were huge and glassy, bright. He made no further move toward her, but he would not back down. Parting ways stirred up an unmistakable sadness in both of them. Yet the longer they stared at each other, the quicker desire returned, and judging by the look in her eye, in Laura, as well.

He lowered his head slightly. "You will probably not believe me, but I missed you," he whispered, eyes dropping to her lips. "I missed knowing where you were, hearing your laughter and love for those boys of ours, your lips against mine. But most of all, I missed talking with you."

"We only argued in the end," she whispered.

"I will always miss you. Laura, we don't—"

Her fingers covered his lips suddenly...and then her lips replaced them.

Nash's knees nearly buckled as his wife, who wanted to divorce him, suddenly kissed him with a passion he'd thought long lost.

He backed toward the bench, sat down, pulling Laura hurriedly onto his lap. He put his arms around her body, and he held her tight against him as he was kissed nearly to breathlessness.

Just as he thought he could take no more, Laura wrenched herself away. She stood before him a moment, staring at him with wide shocked eyes, before she moaned and hitched up her gown and fled from him yet again. Rushing back toward the house, where a thousand mistakes from their past might come between them once more.

He called her name, but she did not stop. Nash watched her go, knowing he had to follow her but afraid to. They had to discuss what that kiss might signify. If they were not done with each other, if passion remained they had a chance to rebuild their life together. He needed to know now before it was too late.

The longer they were together and spoke of their feelings and the past, the further away divorcing seemed to become.

Nash was already struggling with his decision to pursue a divorce. Finding things about Laura he'd misplaced in his mind that had been brought out into the light. Things he'd missed. Things like the scent of her hair, her laugh, the gentleness of her hands on his body, and the certainty that she knew him better than any woman ever could. Not that she liked the things she'd discovered about him.

He had not been the doting husband she deserved. He had let her down badly.

But her passionate nature only needed a little encouragement to blossom. Laura was fighting her desires too, and knowing that they both struggled gave him heart. She might just be his again if he said the right things and put her first, finally.

Could he woo Laura back into his life and this time do a better job of being her husband? Could he repair their marriage and make it better? Because while ever there was passion like that between them, surely it was worth saving.

"Nash?"

He spun about to see Algernon edging toward him slowly through the trees. "Is everything all right? Are you well?"

"Of course I'm well. What are you doing out here? Spying?"

"I'm counting orange trees on the estate to compare with what is recorded by father's last steward." He shrugged and waved a hand at him. "You'd best comb your fingers through your hair and straighten your attire before you're seen again. Anyone might think you were rolling around on the ground."

Nash glanced down at himself, discovering himself in utter disarray. He hastily re-tucked his shirt, buttoned his waistcoat, but his cravat was a sorry mess with no hope of salvation without a mirror.

He ran his fingers through his hair, but gave that up as a lost cause and glanced at his brother again—and saw Algernon was struggling not to smile.

Algernon nodded toward Ravenswood, where Laura could still be seen running away through the garden. "I gather your walk was more productive without my company."

"Shut up," Nash snapped.

"I said nothing to warrant that response," Algernon complained.

"I can always hear what you don't say," he grumbled. Algernon knew that he and Laura had been together. He was almost gloating about it, too.

Algernon sidled closer. "I trust I don't need the hourglass to tell you what to do next?"

Nash turned away from him, thinking of what exactly he should do and it was not to follow his wife immediately. He walked deeper into the orange grove. He could not make demands. He couldn't assume anything when it came to Laura. He had to tread carefully. If she wanted him still, she was not at all comfortable with the discovery.

Algernon chased after him and stopped him in his tracks. "This is the wrong way," he chided.

Nash turned on his brother, sick of his meddling. "Does it ever bother you that you sound just like him sometimes?"

"Sound like him, yes. So do you. Think like him, I try very hard not to. For example, our father would never want you to chase after your wife like I'm urging you to do now."

"Not that. Presuming you are always right. Telling us what to do when you have never been in the same situation."

"I don't need to be in your situation to know what is best for you, brother," Algernon protested. "I swear that I have only your best interests at heart."

"By forcing us to dissect our failure. My failures?"

"That is not at all what I intended. I ask you this now: how can you have three children together and not care about each other? You hovered over Laura during her first pregnancies, and I saw your face, the hurt you couldn't hide, when you realized you'd entirely missed Isabelle's arrival. Your marriage was never about having an heir and spare, in case I did not wed. It was purely for her well-being, and yours. You loved her but you were too young to know how to show it, and Lord knows, Father never encouraged discussion of tender feeling toward women or wives."

"I don't—"

"One more foolish word out of your mouth, Nash, and I will shut it with my fist. You love Laura," Algernon insisted. "You always did, and she loved you."

The last was said softly, gently, and Nash shut his eyes. "If she ever did, she never told me," he whispered.

"Well, you're not the easiest man to care about, are you?" Algernon slapped his shoulder. "You allow no one to make a fuss over you."

"I never noticed Laura try."

"Because she was not allowed to make a single decision around here," Ravenswood claimed, nearly bouncing on his toes. "She tried to be with you but Father couldn't stand to lose his hold over you. Oh, no. Women had no place in the running of Ravenswood after mother died. The only place Laura had you was in the bedroom's privacy, and that was the one place Father never could compete. So he made sure you could hardly be there."

"What do you mean?"

"Look, during the early years of your marriage, I made a point never to dawdle on my way past her bedchamber door. I don't know what went on between you in there, but it certainly made me feel inadequate as a man."

Nash gaped.

"Do you have any idea how special you two were together? How well matched in passion? I would give up my title to find a woman like that to marry."

Nash frowned. "Is that why you hesitate with Lady Stephanie?"

"Well, of course it is. Lady Stephanie is not my match, but she will probably become my duchess. She pretends to enjoy my attentions in order to gain my favor and a proposal. She could never want me the way Laura does you. I doubt Laura ever had to pretend with you."

"Have you bedded Lady Stephanie?"

Algernon shrugged. "She made herself available once, but it was not...good."

Nash had never had an unsatisfactory night with his wife. They had been good in bed together from the start, but that did not necessarily mean they could still be.

"Laura said she doesn't want me anymore," he admitted quietly. "She said she does not want more children, either."

"Surely it is possible to deny yourself to give her the life she wants," Algernon exclaimed. "Curb your lust, dust off your charm, and put it to good use for once. Court Laura and woo your wife back into your arms. But do not make the same mistakes you did last time."

"What were they?"

"Rushing away the next morning to work for the estate. Stay with her. Be a husband during the day, too. When you are in the same room, she watches every move you make, and when you leave, she becomes quiet. Remember what Jasper said upon her return? You can be with her during the day, too."

He fought a blush. "That wasn't what our brother said I should do."

Algernon waved his hand about. "We all know you're a master between the sheets, judging by her screams of ecstasy on past nights. If you take my advice, ignore your doubts—and us, too—

and things will work out in the end. And if your wooing occurs beyond the bedroom, it will be entirely our own fault if we see anything we shouldn't. Never apologize for desiring your wife."

Nash struggled to withhold the grin that his brothers might judge themselves by his standard. It was downright funny, in fact, and he gave up and laughed at the absurdity of Algernon envying him.

"There, that's better. You've been looking far too grim lately. No doubt vexed by still wanting to make love to your wife. And she wants you, too, judging by the state of your clothes today and the speed of her flight, which was quite remark-able." Then Algernon chuckled.

"What's so funny now," Nash demanded to know.

"Five minutes here alone with you in the or-chard where you first met, and she's tearing off your clothes. I really would give all this to have a woman like that in my life."

Nash pursed his lips, seeing the unexpected kiss with greater understanding. To him, this place held special meaning. It was where he must have fallen for Laura.

"Now, I am headed for the stables, and I'll go out riding again," Algernon said. "The servants are with your children. Jasper and Sophie went for a long walk, so you can guess what that means. So that leaves just you and Laura at Ravenswood, more or less alone. Off with you now to find your wife. She's waiting to be swept off her feet at last."

Nash hardly needed his prompting anymore. He wanted his wife back—and by God, he would get into her good graces somehow.

CHAPTER THIRTEEN

LAURA SAVAGED HER THUMB, appalled by her lapse of control around Nash. For heaven's sake, she'd kissed him, started undressing him, and would have gladly been made love to by him in that blasted orange grove.

She could still feel the rush of arousal coursing through her veins after an hour away from him, too. Thank God he had not followed her, expecting more. The need for fulfillment and the frustration of denying herself satisfaction was the frosting on top of a terrible day indeed.

Now Nash knew that she felt attracted toward him still. Knew that if he crooked his finger, she might go running into his arms and his bed once more. This is not how she should behave. Hadn't she told him she was done with husbands and making babies?

The discussion of his proposal had been her undoing, and the devastated look on Nash's face when she explained why she'd chosen to marry him. That hadn't been the only reason she'd said yes, though. She'd grown to care about him before his proposal, and thought she'd gotten to know him from their secret meetings. He was sweet and always respectful toward her. He'd talked to her and never once attempted to take liberties. He hadn't even kissed her until after she'd agreed to marry him. Their first kiss had been in front of their shocked parents.

And then they were married and nothing was as she'd expected. They no longer needed to meet in the orchard, and he became reserved, especially around others.

The only time he seemed comfortable with her was alone in their bedchamber, where they had learned to be intimate together. They were good at making babies...and practicing making them as well.

She glanced across at Thomas and Liam and sighed, her heart filling with love and pride.

The boys took after their parents. Thomas too serious and Liam bound for mischief, like she had been. Isabelle she wasn't sure about but she loved to laugh.

Now and then, when Nash looked at their

daughter, he seemed so sad. She didn't think his sadness was over Isabelle's existence, though, but for all the things he'd missed in her life so far. He'd been present for the birth of their sons, but not Isabelle's. He'd been considerate and concerned about Laura's welfare during and immediately after her first pregnancies.

But as soon as she proved herself fit and healthy, the demands of the duke had taken him away from her repeatedly. That hadn't entirely been his fault. She understood better now the pressure he'd been under. The torment his father had inflicted still had a hold over him from the grave.

She raised her face to the heavens and cursed under her breath. Her decisions had been easily made at a distance from Nash. She had imagined her attraction to him would go away. Yet, she still wanted him to make love to her today, even with the risk of bearing him a fourth child. But that went against all logic and sensibility. If she gave in to passion, she would never be free of her husband or their marriage. She would be bound forever to this place.

Nash might never change, and she no longer expected he would try.

Not for her.

Not for them.

Not even for himself. He was satisfied with the way he was.

"Mama?"

She turned to look at her oldest child. "Yes, Thomas."

"What are you thinking about?"

A lost cause. "I thought that it's high time we got out of here."

"Where can we go?"

Far away. Somewhere they could play without rules and objections. "I don't know. Where would you like to go?"

"To find Papa," Thomas announced. "I want to show him my new drawing."

Laura's smile became difficult to maintain. She couldn't see Nash yet, she was not fully in control of herself. She hadn't the faintest idea what to say to him to ensure he wouldn't take advantage of her lapse.

"Your papa is here," Nash said, strolling in with his arms full of a tea tray. He set it down on the floor and the children squealed with delight, rushing over to see what he'd brought for them.

"I had the cook prepare a surprise for everyone," he murmured, going to their daughter and lifting her up high. Isabelle laughed, and he brought her down to cuddle, and then looked into her eyes with utter adoration shining in his own. "Let's see what your favorite might be, little one."

Nash sat down on the floor before the tray, long legs crossed under him as if he did it every day. He looked so odd and large beside the boys, but he plopped Isabelle onto his lap, acting as if nothing had happened between them earlier. "Mama, will you join us?"

She was too stunned by Nash and his nonchalant behavior to answer immediately, of course. But she soon found her tongue. "Of course I will."

"Good." He made a space at his side for her to sit and poured her a cup of tea. On the tray was an assortment of little cakes and five oranges.

He spoke only with their sons while he tried to tempt Isabelle to eat cake more daintily. The boys laughed at the mess their sister made, and Nash kept smiling, too, but kept trying to instill some manners in the girl. He soon gave up put Isabelle down on the floor beside him, letting her crawl away to find a toy that had caught her eye.

He watched their daughter with a captivated expression on his face and absently reached for an orange. "She'll grow up to be as quick as your mother, and Mama can run fast when the occasion calls for it."

He did not look her way as he peeled the oranges, but she knew he was talking about her earlier flight from the orchard.

She was not amused by his teasing. She saw

running away as yet another sign of her weakness about him. If she didn't care for him, she should have walked away, not run. Yet when it came to Nash, her emotions were always too close to the surface.

But she did care about him, and what he thought of her, too. It annoyed that, despite being unwilling to live with him, she was desperate to prove his power over her desires had waned in the years they'd been apart. The push and pull of her attraction and conflicting desire to leave him was giving her quite the headache.

She rubbed her brow.

Nash held out the orange to her, peeled and ready for her consumption. "I recall you used to like these best of all."

"I still do, but I'm not hungry."

A tiny smile appeared on his lips, but Isabelle returned, and he devoted himself to offering her a segment of orange. Their daughter spat it out, and Nash laughed, setting that piece aside. He pursed his lips, perusing the remaining choices on the plates. "How about we try my favorite, then? See what you think of shortbread instead."

Isabelle gobbled that up, humming, and reached for more. Nash chuckled. "A girl after my heart. Always after the sweetest treat on offer."

His eyes flickered toward Laura, and she felt

an answering blush warm her cheeks. Thankfully, Nash looked away again and devoted himself to eating and talking with their three children like the doting parent she'd always wanted him to be.

His hand suddenly settled on her leg, just above her knee, and then just as swiftly disappeared. Her breath caught at the contact between them.

She wanted to move away but couldn't seem to uncurl her legs from beneath her.

Eventually, the tea ended and the children went back to their own interests. Nash turned Isabelle to face him. "You know, despite your atrocious lack of manners, you are exactly like your mother. Adorable."

"Wait till she screams at you or cries all night long," she warned.

"Something I look forward to, given all I've missed already." He handed Isabelle to her and rose to his feet in one smooth motion. When he reached down for the girl again, their hands brushed, but he didn't offer to help Laura up.

He took Isabelle away to find her a new toy to play with, leaving Laura sitting on the floor alone, watching them all.

Isabelle wriggled to be let down from Nash's arms, and he obliged but stood leaning against a wall, watching her with a fascinated expression on his face. He seemed quite taken by their daughter. He also seemed to want to get to know her in a way he had not with their sons at first, and that pleased Laura. She'd not expected him to display any affection for the girl so quickly. She had expected him to ignore her for quite some time.

When his expression turned brooding, Laura felt guilt. She had robbed Nash of an important part of the girl's life. If things had been different he would have been there for the birth and the first to hold their new child. She could never make that up to him. After a moment of consideration, she got to her feet, excused herself and slipped from the room.

In her chambers, she found the journal she'd kept of her pregnancy, through the third month of Isabelle's life. She hadn't known why she'd written everything down. She had not thought to keep a journal when she'd carried her sons. But she'd been lonely and living with near strangers, in a strange place, so she'd taken to writing her thoughts about the small events in her days.

She'd started off angry with herself and Nash, and full of regret too, without knowing why or who she was writing for. But she thought she knew now who might want to read her journal. She would give it to Nash now. It might help him deal with his shock and answer some of his questions about becoming a father again.

She held it close and glanced at the door to the hall.

No, she couldn't put it in his hands in front of the children, because she'd have to explain. It might be cowardly, but she would leave it on his bed for him to find later tonight, after he'd retired.

She steeled herself and approached the connecting doorway to his room. She'd spent no significant time in his chambers. She'd not been invited, and she'd never asked why. Nash had preferred to come to her room, and he'd always been out of bed at first light, much earlier than she had liked to rise.

She put her hand on the latch. It swung open silently.

Nash's room was of similar proportions to hers, but much more masculine. Dark wood paneling, rich dark blue curtained bed. Neatness everywhere.

She walked toward the bed and placed her journal on a pillow. Overwhelmed by the scent of his cologne on the air, she trembled and turned on her heel to leave, only to stop when she saw her own face. It wasn't a reflection, but a small drawing hanging on the wall between their two chambers.

Laura didn't remember posing for any drawings during her marriage. Had never known Nash to have commissioned one, either. As far as she knew, there had never been an image of her created by anyone in his family, or even her own.

But it was a remarkable likeness, catching her in an unguarded moment seated by a window. The setting was indistinct, and she appeared quite young, so it must have been done some time ago. But why hadn't Nash told her about the drawing? Shown her? Why hang it there?

Well, she supposed she didn't know about it because there was so much they'd not talked about still.

She couldn't take her eyes from it as she left the room though. Nash had kept a memento of her, hung it opposite his bed, where he had seen it every day...and unlike his wedding band, had still not removed it?

Laura rubbed her brow, feeling her headache worsen. She could not understand why Nash did the things the way he did them.

Coming home and demanding a divorce was not going at all as she'd expected. She was seeing a side of Nash she'd never seen before. He wasn't as reserved as he'd once been with the children. Their talks with the duke had scratched open old wounds and revealed he was vulnerable to sentiment, but he had kept secrets about his life that a wife should have known about long ago.

She left his room, still pondering why Nash would keep a drawing of her in his room when he claimed to want to divorce her. She glanced down at her bare finger and grimaced at the absence of the only gift he'd ever given her that had mattered to her.

She curled her fingers into a fist, determined not to regret removing her wedding ring. Though there had been advantages to wearing one on her finger all these years. People assumed her husband was never far away, or traveling, and she had allowed them to think so for her protection.

But she'd never really been protected from the genuine danger—the late Duke of Ravenswood's. He was gone though, and she was no longer in fear for her life.

But she would be cut adrift from the family soon though and had to depend on herself for protection in the future. Yet where once that might have gladdened her heart, now it only made it beat faster with a sense of dread.

Nash would remarry, of course.

He did nothing without reason, and the most likely one was to take a second wife with another fortune to share with his family. He was far too young to spend his remaining years as chastely as she planned to spend hers.

A knock sounded on her door, and she hurried into her room, quietly shutting the door to Nash's chamber before she answered her own.

A servant was waiting. "The duke wishes for your company again, my lady."

She nodded, resigned to yet another turning of the hourglass, as she fought this time to ignore her nervousness about what the future held in store.

CHAPTER FOURTEEN

NASH HAD NEVER KNOWN Laura kept a journal until he found the one sitting on his pillow last night. It was not inscribed with her name or dated, but he recognized her handwriting immediately.

He had read through the first pages a few times, trying to get a sense of when it began and why she'd left it for him to find. There was no mention of who had helped her escape Ravenswood, or where she had gone to live.

It began with her surprise at discovering she was with child as his only reference point.

She had been uncommonly ill. Casting up her accounts day and night but still craving cake at odd hours like she had with their first two children. She mentioned a baker lived not far away, which meant she must have lived in a good-sized town. There were gaps in time where nothing of note must have happened. But she had begun each entry with the number of weeks since her condition became apparent, or perhaps the number represented the time since they had made love.

Either way, it gave him a clue how she had spent her days. She had not been happy, he soon discovered. Her journal did not suggest any great pleasure in her days. Just mentioned the passage of time. Bare of emotion, which told him she was troubled. Laura was always emotional. Occasionally she wrote about missing her mama's advice and the comfort of familiar surroundings.

When he reached entries later in the journal, there was a mention of the expense of a midwife, and it became clear that she was living under someone's charity. She spoke of a debt that could never be repaid. And then...

My Isabelle was born last Sunday. Healthy and precious, but of course, being her mama, I am entirely biased. Despite my happiness in her arrival, I have cried endlessly every day since her birth like before but worse this time, knowing I will have no choice but to give her up.

There were more entries after that, but he could not bear to continue reading them.

He clenched his jaw and closed the book carefully. He should have been with Laura before that birth. She'd been moody and her spirits had sunk after the birth of each of their sons, too. Many women suffered the same, he'd since heard.

Nash had done all he could to reassure her that all was well then, but he'd not been with her for Isabella's arrival, and she'd only had the company of strangers.

He should have gone after Laura. He would have torn the world apart to reach her had he known of her pregnancy. He should never have let her out of his sight for as long as he had. Never trusted his father either. He should have done a great many things differently. But he could not change the past any more than he could fly.

He rubbed his tired eyes. He'd been reading all night. Unable to put down the journal until he'd read every word.

"Brother, are you crying?" Jasper whispered, standing at the doorway of his bedchamber. He wore a worried expression. "Do you have bad news or is that just a sad tale you've been reading?"

Nash brushed his face, realizing he had indeed been crying. He set the book under his pillow, deciding he would read it again later, and wiped away his tears. "Yes, it was sad."

"What was it?"

He turned to Jasper and ignored the question. "Did you want something?"

Jasper held up his hands. "I just stopped by to say we are leaving for London. Algernon recommends some haste in our marriage, and Sophie, too, is eager to be wed and with her friends present. We wanted to say our goodbyes before…"

"Before what?"

Jasper winced. "Before Laura disappears from our lives again."

Nash burst to his feet. "She will not disappear this time."

"I'm glad to hear that. Will you come down to see us off? Sophie is waiting for us downstairs."

"Yes, of course."

He followed his brother down the main staircase, looking for signs of Laura and the children. He'd not heard them today and that was now unusual.

"So, you will let Laura return to see the children?"

"The duke has not agreed to support the divorce yet," he said slowly.

"Well, not in so many words, but I'm sure he will. He always sides with you in the end," Jasper murmured with a shake of his head. "Even when you are wrong."

"He does not," he warned as they reached the entrance hall. If he had, Nash would not be feeling so wretched this morning. He had made so many mistakes he could never correct. "There have been plenty of occasions when we simply could not be bothered arguing with each other. We had enough of that with Father."

"We all did. So, is she leaving or not?" Jasper asked. "I mean, if there is any doubt or a reason to hope, I would be glad to know she will be remaining here and we've no need to rush back to wipe away those poor children's tears."

Nash blanched and his stomach pitted with dread. He did not want to think about that possibility because it might not be just them in tears. "Where will you take Sophie first in London?"

"To the theater, perhaps even to a ball if she wishes to dance. But definitely to the pleasure gardens and Bond Street. Anywhere she wants to go, really."

"Anywhere?"

"Well, yes. I've had enough of making my own decisions and doing everything alone. My own company bores me now."

He smiled quickly, but Jasper's words were like a knife to the heart, opening his mind to the possibilities of conducting a second courtship of his wife. It was hard to woo someone in a place with so many bad memories for one of them and little to do.

He could take Laura to London next season, but he didn't care for the idea of leaving his sons and daughter behind. He'd grown accustomed to knowing where they were. All of them. Laura especially. If they went to London, he could take her and the children to the menagerie, or sailing on the Thames, or even attend some picnics together during the day if Laura thought it a good idea.

The London town house could fit them all. But he would have to purchase some new toys to entertain his daughter. After all, there were likely not any toys for girls there and there were precious few here.

He should buy his daughter a pretty new doll.

And it was not as if he was needed here anymore. Algernon and Jasper were working well together to rebuild the future of the estate according to his plan, and although Jasper would spend time in London with his new bride he would return to the estate eventually.

Algernon caught up with them on the stairs. "I have an invitation to dine with the Fairmont family next month, but I plan to be unavailable. They have an unmarried daughter I would like to avoid. Would you care to attend in my place?"

"A pity it's not a ball," Jasper grumbled, taking up the invitation to read it. "The Fairmont's do drag out their dinners until our backsides grow numb on those hard wooden chairs. I shall decline as well, and it is such a relief that we might still be in London then, too."

Nash reached for the invitation, thinking of attending with Laura, but Algernon held it back from him.

"You won't enjoy yourself if you go."

"Why not?"

"Guildford is sure to attend."

That name now set his teeth on edge. "I don't have to speak with him."

"But Laura surely will. Will that bother you?"

He blew out a breath. "Don't be daft," Nash snapped. "Unless you're looking to break another side table."

Algernon put his hands up in mock surrender.

"It is only polite to speak with our neighbors," Laura claimed, joining them, without Isabelle perched on her hip but the boys following. "Where is Sophie?"

"She'll be along at any moment," Jasper promised. "Well..."

Jasper hugged each of them in turn and then turned to Laura. "I hope to return to find you still here when I get back," he said to her.

She winced and embraced Jasper. "Try to behave for once."

Jasper laughed. "Never fear, I've Sophie to keep me in line now, dear sister."

"Poor Sophie," Laura said with a laugh, "She'll have her hands full with you."

"That's my plan," he said winking cheekily.

Nash drew back as the children surged forward to hug their uncle and Sophie strolled in carrying Isabelle. "I hate to leave her."

Jasper snatched the child from her, tickled the girl, and thrust her at Algernon. "Best keep a close eye on this one or she might take her with us."

They all laughed.

Laura wandered over to a window and sat on a window seat. Nash joined her. Puzzled by something. "Why did you not consider Jasper?"

Laura shook her head. "And be teased mercilessly every moment of every day?"

"You have a point."

"And Guildford?"

"I never considered him," she promised, scowling.

"But was he courting you?"

Laura stared straight ahead and he sighed when she didn't answer.

He lowered his voice. "I had heard he might have been a beau of yours."

She rubbed her arm. "Who told you that?"

"Who do you think?"

Laura stilled, and then her eyes turned toward him. "I have never, ever, allowed anyone but you to kiss me."

Nash regarded his wife. There were so many things they'd never talked about yet. Father had filled his ears with so many rumors and innuendo's that he'd taken few seriously. But secrets could easily fester into distrust. "You kissed him."

Laura blanched. But there was no escaping the look of shame that crossed her face. His heart sank. There had been something.

She gulped. "That happened before our engagement."

"So you *did* kiss him?"

"No. He kissed *me*." Laura shuddered. "I never wanted that kiss, if you could call it such a thing."

She glanced about the room before continuing. "Guildford took me by surprise. He grabbed me by my head and forced his lips upon mine. My lip was cut in the process."

Nash sucked in a breath, incensed. "Where were you when this kiss happened?"

"In the lane between my home and his estate. I had dropped my handkerchief somewhere and went back alone to search for it. He had it and wouldn't give it back."

Nash scowled. He and Laura had become

engaged just before her eighteenth birthday. "How old were you?"

"Fifteen, and not out. I knew if I said anything, I might end up married to him, and I did not want that."

Nash curled his hand into a fist at his side. "Did anything else happen I should know about?"

"No. I ran home, and I didn't trust Guildford after that. I avoided him for some time. But before we became engaged, he started coming around again. Pretending to call on my father for his health but always attempting to catch me on the grounds alone. I never encouraged him. That's why I started walking in the other direction, to the orchard where I met you."

"Father knew all about Guildford's interest somehow but he claimed you kissed him," Nash told her, irritated that aspersions had been cast on Laura's character when she was blameless.

"Your father lied a great deal."

Jasper suddenly rushed to the windows overlooking the front drive and cursed out loud. "Damn it all. Guildford just arrived in the drive on horseback and brought someone with him."

"I'll let him wait in the library while we see you off," Algernon announced. He glanced across at Nash. "Do continue this. Get it all out now."

Nash studied his wife, and his heart ached

for her obvious embarrassment that his brothers had heard her every word about Guildford. She should have told him long ago though. He should have been here all these years to protect her from scoundrels like him and stop the other rumors starting. "Tell me the rest."

She gulped again. "After Thomas was born, Guildford came to call on me here a few times when you were gone. He had developed an interest in medicine and presumed to instruct me in matters of women's health and nursing my child. Your father found us sitting too close together one day—Guildford moved toward *me*, not the other way round—and I could tell he assumed I encouraged him. You went away again, and whenever I tried not to be at home to Guildford, the duke would insist I meet with him. I think he wanted me to be unfaithful to you, giving you grounds for an annulment or divorce."

"Laura's dowry would remain with you under those circumstances, wouldn't it Nash," Jasper asked, drawing closer as Algernon returned to the room.

"It would have." Nash shooed him away with a glare, remembering how Father had presented Laura's character in the worst possible light right until the day he died. Father had believed divorce was Nash's only option, ordering him to make haste to marry again afterward and to choose a more obedient bride this time. "Infidelity would certainly have been grounds."

"But Guildford's interest in me was also in pursuit of furthering his study," Laura whispered.

"He's a charlatan's knowledge at best of healing. He had many ideas I disapproved of," he murmured.

"And many more your father agreed with." Laura shivered. "The way Guildford looks at me always makes me uncomfortable. I'm no specimen to be studied."

"Clearly he thought you were if he comes to call on you after each child is born," Jasper cut in.

She shivered again and inched closer to Nash just as the knocker sounded on the front door. After a moment the butler entered the room and whispered urgently to Algernon. The duke frowned at him. "What could he possibly want? Is someone unwell?"

"No, your grace," the butler promised. "Mr. Levinson invited himself to enquire after Lady Sweet's health of his own accord."

Laura recoiled and he put his arm around her in concern for her reaction. "Was it Levinson that bled you?"

"Yes. Your father stood over him and watched."

"Well, he'll never touch you again, I swear."

Laura let out a shaky breath and relaxed

deeper into his embrace. "Send them away," she whispered.

"My brother will," he promised, glancing at his older brother who nodded his agreement.

"Yes, I will deal with the leech with great pleasure," Algernon promised.

Jasper rubbed his hands together. "About time."

"Do not get carried away, Jasper," Nash warned.

Jasper frowned. "But they hurt her? Guildford must know all about it, too."

"There are other ways to put them in their place," the duke promised.

"Spoilsport," Jasper grumbled kissed his future bride on the cheek and followed the duke from the room.

Sophie remained behind, looking worried.

Laura placed her hand on Nash's chest. "Perhaps you should go with them. I don't want trouble stirred up on my behalf."

He caught her hand and raised it to his lips, kissing her bare fingers. "They deserve whatever comes their way but I would not dream of giving them the satisfaction of thinking themselves our equal and fighting them. Algernon will make them suffer in more subtle ways. They are not worth you worrying over anymore so please put them from your mind."

She sighed and leaned a little harder into him. Nash smiled and dared not move.

"What will you do?"

"Whatever you want me to do," he said and then drew Laura to her feet and led her to his former governess and their daughter. "Mrs. Radcliff I wish you and Jasper a safe journey and I look forward to your return as a member of our family," he said and then took Isabelle into his arms. "Tell Jasper to take his time returning from London."

Laura said her goodbyes too and embraced the woman as she wished her a happy marriage and a safe journey as well.

Nash drew Laura away when there seemed no more to say and they strolled into the long hall together.

Laura headed directly toward the nearest staircase and he followed. At the stairs she waited for him but she looked nervous.

"I am sorry I was not here to protect you from Levinson's doctoring."

She inclined her head.

"I want to see what was done," he whispered. "But only when you are ready to show me." Nash leaned over and pressed a kiss to her brow. "There's no good reason to hide them from me."

"There is every reason to hide the ugliness of them from everyone," she said, shivering.

"Nothing about you could ever be ugly," he promised. "You are beautiful, inside and out."

She swayed toward him a moment and then exhaled a shaky breath. "My lord it *is* well past time for Isabelle's nap, don't you think?"

He noticed her attempt to change the subject and allowed it. "Yes, I think she must be."

Nash urged the boys up the last flight and told them to head toward the nursery. "Turn back her bedding and wait for us there," he called after them.

Then he set his free arm around Laura as they began to climb the last steep set. Laura did not try to remove him until they reached the landing close to the nursery. She moved out of reach suddenly and sighed. "I would like to be alone for a while."

Nash lowered his head to hide his disappointment. He understood she was upset about their visitors but he did not like the idea of separation very much. "Shall I put Isabelle to bed for you?"

She nodded. "I'd appreciate you trying."

Nash had watched Laura enough to have learned her way with the girl. "Will you join the children and I for luncheon?"

"I..."

"We will wait for however long it takes."

She nodded again and Nash went to her again. He put his fingers under her chin and raised her face to his. "I *will* protect you from now on. You have nothing to fear here."

He waited a beat and then kissed her softly on the lips right there in the hall.

Laura allowed it, but as soon as he lifted his head she started down the stairs again. Nash quickly went to the balustrade and watched her decent. He had surprised his wife by kissing her again but he had meant it only to seal his vow. Her health and her safety, her needs, came first with him now, as it should have done all along. "You know where I will be when you need me," he called out to her. "Don't be away too long."

CHAPTER FIFTEEN

LAURA STILLED Liam as he wriggled in her arms. "Are you ready?"

"No."

"Don't be afraid. I'm here with you," she promised her youngest son. "You can do this."

Laura stood above the stream of rushing water on an overhanging ledge, legs bared to her knees, with her dress pinned up so she could dunk her youngest son into the deeper pool in front of them. She released him and he fell, only to spring back up immediately.

Laura hurried to the shallows as he spluttered and paddled back toward her, keeping his head above water as she'd told him to do several times already. Liam was no longer afraid to have water cover his face, not as he had been the first time she'd thrown him in that day.

He was gaining confidence but tiring, and he

was also laughing in a way that made her heart sing. She truly had missed her sons' voices. Their small successes made her feel complete.

Liam was learning to swim much faster than she'd expected and enjoying their time together away from the palace.

For a change, Nash had decided not to join them but was expected eventually. She was glad of that. He agreed with her that swimming lessons were called for while the weather was good. He would join them when Isabelle woke from her daily nap.

Liam stood when he reached the shallower water. "Can we do it again?"

"All right, but this is the last time." She stepped back up onto the ledge. "Your mama is getting tired arms." Liam raised his once again, and she lifted him up high. "Goodness, you've gotten so much heavier since we started today. I swear the water is making you grow."

She glanced quickly to one side. Thomas was watching them from the shore but had declined to take part in her lessons with Liam. She was sorry about that. He'd been like Liam when she'd taught him all those years ago. Always wanting to be thrown in just one more time. Always laughing.

He did not do that often enough now.

Her leaving had changed him, turned him almost as serious as his father could be.

Laura heaved Liam out into the water, and he disappeared under the surface one last time. She watched the water until his head popped up and then ordered him to swim toward Thomas, where the bottom was sandy and much shallower.

She joined him there and sat on a boulder in the shallows, enjoying the wash of water across her calves. "You're going to be an excellent swimmer, Liam. As good as your brother."

"No, he won't be as good as me. I'm always better because I'm the eldest," Thomas announced and strode off toward the deeper water.

She shot to her feet. "Thomas, come back here."

"No. I can jump in myself and swim," he insisted, hands on his hips. "I don't need to be thrown in like a baby."

She pursued him, but it was far too late to stop him. He dove in.

When he came up, he was spluttering badly, and he immediately sank down again.

Before Laura could wade in to rescue him, Nash passed her by and caught up their son in his arms.

He lifted Thomas above the waterline as he continued to cough and splutter. Laura let out a sigh of relief that no harm had come to their eldest.

But that relief disappeared as she heard what Nash was saying to Thomas, and the force behind his words made her wince.

Thomas was cowering and squirming to escape his father's grasp.

Nash had lost his temper, though the danger had passed.

Laura hurried to the edge of the water and reached for her son. "Give him to me."

"No. He deliberately disobeyed you, and it will not be tolerated. He could have drowned, and you too, if you'd gone in deeper wearing that heavy gown."

Thomas looked about to cry from the scolding, and she held out her hands again.

"But he didn't drown, Nash. We wouldn't have let that happen." She waded in deeper put her hand on Nash's shoulder. "This is between Thomas and me now. Go back to shore and dry off with Liam."

"But—"

She gave his shoulder a harder squeeze. "*Please*, Nash. Go. It's important."

He looked down at her hand on his shoulder, and Laura slowly withdrew her touch.

"Very well," he murmured, and made his way back to shore and to Liam.

She studied her eldest son until he squirmed. He'd been scolded enough by his father, but he was in no immediate danger of drowning now. She gestured to bring him closer. "When was the last time you came to the pool?"

Thomas mumbled, "With you."

Years ago. She brushed his wet hair back from his eyes and winced. "Until your father and I are sure you're ready to swim alone again, you will not disobey me. You upset your father and frightened me. Now, do it properly this time."

Thomas' glance strayed to the shoreline. "But Papa said—"

"I'm watching you, and I be right here if you need help again," she promised.

As he hurried to comply, she glanced at the shoreline. Nash had risen to his feet, but she held her hand out to him, keeping him at bay. Then she watched Thomas hesitate at the edge.

Nash had inadvertently made him afraid of water.

"Jump," she ordered, determined to get him past his awkwardness before it became an embedded fear.

Eventually, he did jump and came up quickly, with only a small gasp for air this time. She smiled in relief and tried to hug him as he joined her, but he avoided her touch. "Well done, my dear boy. Now do ten more."

Thomas groaned, but he did as she asked. When he was done, they turned for the shore to see Nash and Liam standing there watching. Nash had removed his sodden coat, waistcoat and his shoes. She barely recognized him. But he was clearly unhappy still. She raised a brow at Nash, gesturing at Thomas until he finally understood.

"Well done, son," he called, nodding.

Liam, sensing an end to the tension, rushed toward his brother, promising when he was big enough he would dive in that many times, too. Laura left them to play in the shallows a bit longer and went to her husband's side.

"I lost my temper," he admitted, looking sheepish.

"Yes, I think you did a bit, but no harm was done."

"I should know better." Nash grimaced. "When Stratford heard his friend nearly drowned, he developed such a fear of water, he wouldn't come here with us anymore."

"Yes, I heard about Winston, and that was why I insisted Thomas learn to swim when he was young."

"I shouldn't have yelled the way I did," Nash admitted, rubbing a hand over his wet and now curly hair.

"He frightened you."

"That is no excuse for losing my temper. He's just a child."

"We all say things in the heat of the moment that we sometimes wish we'd never said," she offered.

"That is true," he said slowly, then looked at her sideways. "Did you swim today?"

She hadn't and didn't want to explain why so she ignored the question. "Where is Isabelle?"

"Algernon has her. I went to talk to him about ending our discussions."

"How did it go?"

"Pointless in the end," he said, sighing. "I asked him to put an end to the meetings, but he refuses to see sense."

"It makes him feel like he's in control," she decided. "But he's not."

"No. On that, we can agree." Nash glanced her way again and suddenly smiled. "I think I'll swim."

"Very well."

He peeled off his linen shirt, revealing a rather well-muscled physique. Laura could barely drag her eyes away from him and a blush heated her cheeks.

Nash noticed. "Care to join me?"

"No. I will return the children indoors for those lessons you always prattle on about and rescue Isabelle from the duke."

"Don't go back yet," he muttered. "Wait for me."

Nash was a strong swimmer, unlike many men his age seemed to be. He'd always been moving, rushing hither and yon at the duke's behest. Such a life of activity and challenge had suited him. Kept him fit. But he'd never seemed able to relax completely.

"All right, I will wait."

He strode off, hoisting the children under his arms and jumping into the deep water with them shrieking.

Laura followed the trio along the bank a little way but eventually stopped to watch them clown about at a distance. Liam soon paddled back toward her and the shallows and got out again.

But Nash and Thomas remained swimming in the depths, whispering together. Soon Nash had Thomas in his arms and they floated off downstream in the slow current with a cheery wave.

An unexpected sigh escaped her lips. Clearly, Nash could be sweet and even impulsive. But the chances of that occurring around her had always been less often than she'd liked. Seeing him now with Thomas in the water reminded her of all the things she'd hoped they'd be as husband and wife and as a family.

Liam tugged her sleeve. "I'm cold."

"Oh, of course, darling. We'll wrap you tight in a blanket and dry you off again. The other pair will not be too long, I expect."

"Yes, Mama."

He left first, and she remained behind a moment, watching her husband and son drift away on the slow-moving current. The increasing distance gave her a feeling of panic, until she chided herself that she was being foolish. Nash would let no harm come to Thomas.

She kept her attention on her youngest son and hurried to remove his wet garments, scrub him dry and dress him in the fresh, dry garments she'd brought with them.

When she was done, he hugged her without saying a word. Laura sat down on a blanket and was nearly brought to tears when Liam crawled into her lap like the baby he'd been when she'd left him behind.

"Can we come here tomorrow?"

"Not tomorrow. I hope to see how you sit a horse tomorrow."

"I don't like horses as much as Thomas does," Liam admitted.

"Well, I still want to see you on one just the same." She neatened his hair with her fingers and he leaned into her touch. "Don't fret, I'll be watching over you."

He caught her hand and wrapped it around himself. "I'd like that."

Laura was nearly moved to tears again by the way Liam had accepted her back into his life. He was the most sensitive of her sons and the only one who sought her out for affection. She regretted that she would have to leave him soon.

When she looked up, it was to see Thomas walking toward her shivering from the cold, with Nash bringing up the rear.

She gently removed Liam from her lap and gathered up a cloth so Thomas could dry off. But he refused her help. She stood awkwardly to one side as he struggled to dry himself unaided. She passed him a change of clothes piece by piece, and he turned away from her to dress himself each time.

A small hand crept into hers and squeezed. Laura clung to Liam, struggling not to feel slighted by her firstborn. At least one of her sons still wanted her around. Not that she could blame Thomas for punishing her in the only way a child could. He'd learned to do without her.

Thomas rushed off toward the manor, talking Liam into going with him. She sighed and shook her head. She might never regain Thomas' trust, and that was her fault entirely.

Nash cleared his throat. "Your skirts, Laura."

She glanced down. In her preoccupation

with dressing Liam and then Thomas, she'd completely forgotten to remove the pins from her skirts. She was currently displaying a lot of leg—and her husband was definitely taking in the view.

Unfortunately, the pins refused to yield. A blush heated her cheeks as she struggled and failed. "I'll be along in a minute. Go on ahead without me."

"No. Let me see."

"No. I don't need you!" She drew in a shaking breath, knowing that her anger was not for Nash but for herself. "Forgive me."

He sighed. "You've made it abundantly clear you don't need me, but the gown does unless you wish to create a hole in the garment."

She huffed and threw her hands up in defeat. "Fine."

Nash approached, still bare chested, and sank to one knee before her. His shoulder muscles rippled as his hands rose to touch her skirts and he gently removed pin after pin, turning her around slowly to do so.

His hands brushed downward, straightening her skirts to the ground before she could think to do it herself. Somehow, his fingers even brushed against her ankle, and she shivered from the chill of his touch.

He looked up slowly.

She held her breath as Nash rose until her face was level with his wide chest. He had gooseflesh on his skin. "You're cold."

"I don't feel it. Not around you."

She had to force her gaze up to meet his.

Their eyes held for too long and a flush of warmth swept over her body.

Nash did not move back, and Laura could barely breathe for the rising tension stirring between them now.

"I wish you had joined me in the water," Nash whispered, and his fingers settled softly at her waist. "The boys shouldn't have been the only ones enjoying a swim."

"It's not important."

His eyes narrowed. "It is to me. I want you to enjoy being here with us again," he said quietly. "With me as well. I would have liked to see you out of that dress, too."

She gasped.

"I won't apologize for saying that." He looked away. "You're my wife and you've a fine figure. I would like to see it by the light of day once before..."

Before they divorced.

Laura turned away from Nash, aware of him as a man she found desirable still and who clearly still desired her. It was unsettling how lust remained and how easy it might be to give in to those feelings.

She still longed to feel his body against her own one last time, too. But of course, it was far too late for that.

Nash's hand settled on her shoulder, warmer now and compelling, but when she flinched, he moved past her to gather up his wet clothes without another word.

She exhaled, believing the moment of weakness was over. He pulled only his fine linen shirt over his head, but it was still wet and clung to the bunched muscles of his upper arms and torso. Laura tried not to stare.

"Laura. While you are here, I want to know everything you do and think. I don't wish to end our marriage with secrets and anger in our hearts."

"If Algernon has his way, he will know all our secrets as well," she complained.

"We could just sit together next time and say nothing to his questions. He can't really punish us for failing to answer him."

"But he might not support our divorce," she argued.

"There are things that happened between us that should remain our memories alone," Nash insisted. "We should also talk soon about what you will do after you leave."

"Why?"

"Because I care about what will become of you. You are the mother of my children and you've been part of my life for nearly half of it now. That's longer than even my mother had been."

His confession surprised her to the point of speechlessness. Never once had she ever believed they could be each other's confidants. But now at the end, Nash suddenly wanted to be.

He was the only constant in her life, too. "Very well. We shall give the duke the silent treatment next time and see how he takes it."

"Not well, most likely," Nash said with an unexpected grin. "But he always told us brothers that adversity builds character."

"I should enjoy seeing him frustrated for a change."

"It's not pretty." He laughed and gestured toward the manor, and they continued their walk after the children. After a few yards of silence, Nash turned to her. "I want to talk to you about the night Isabelle was conceived again."

She felt her cheeks warming.

"What were you thinking, approaching me in such a place, in such a way? What if it hadn't been me in the dark but a stranger?"

"But it *was* you."

"It was so dark in my corner of the room, I could barely see you!"

"But that's how we were always together. In the dark of my room. You always found me, and I always found you."

She had been lonely the night they'd made Isabelle, and tired of being alone for the longest time as well. Hearing her husband had had a great time attending balls and parties like the masquerade without her during that season had made her reckless.

When she'd seen him regarding other women as they'd passed him by, her temper had gotten the better of her. He was *her* husband, not some other woman's plaything. She'd stepped toward his shadowed corner, and he'd seen her, and with one crook of his finger, her sensibilities had flown away.

Nash caught her eye. "It was good between us that night, wasn't it?"

"Yes," she admitted slowly.

"I felt a connection that I've never experienced with anyone but you."

"So, there *were* other women?"

"No. I wanted no one but you from the day we met. And what of you?"

"You know me."

The corner of his lips lifted. "Do I?"

"I've no interest in men."

Nash growled. "Don't lie."

"I'm not. I've never once imagined another man in my bed."

He paused, spearing her with a hard glance. "Have you imagined *me* since our separation? Did you dream of me in your bed?"

Laura pressed her lips together. The existence of their third child proved she had wanted her husband at least once more. "Yes."

"Good. I want to have you again," he said.

"*Have me?* You mean visit my bedchamber, part ways each morning, and never speak until it's time to make love again?"

"We are speaking of now, not the past," Nash said and began to walk again.

"If it wasn't for your wish for divorce, and Algernon with his wretched hourglass, nothing would have changed between us. You can't have a wife and keep her at arm's length. I won't have it. We are over."

Nash's hand whipped out and hauled her close. "We are not over, and I have precious little time left to prove I deserve your trust. It is *you* holding *me* at arm's length now, Laura, but if anyone visits anyone's bedchamber, it must be you coming to mine at last. Something you never once did when we were first married. I always had to come to you."

Laura shook off his grip. "I was never welcome in your chambers. Your valet locked the door between our rooms each morning and unlocked it at night just before you came into mine."

Nash stared at her, clearly shocked. "I never told him to do that."

"Well, someone did," she growled. "I told you everyone here was against me."

"It was never meant to be that way," Nash promised, shaking his head.

A bead of water slid down his cheek, and her hand itched to wipe it away. She defeated the urge and shook her head. "You will break my heart all over again when the novelty of a wife wears off again and you go away. I can't live like that."

"You won't have to," he shot back. "I promise."

"I've heard that before, and you still left."

"Mama?"

Laura spun about quickly to see her eldest son had returned watching them argue with wide eyes. She forced a smile to her face when she saw his expression. "Yes, Thomas?"

He pointed toward home. "Liam stubbed his toe and won't stop crying about it. He wants someone to carry him home. He wants you."

Laura hitched up her skirts and rushed to her

youngest son, who was sitting on the ground some distance away, hugging his foot and wailing.

For a change, Nash did not attempt to take over.

CHAPTER SIXTEEN

"LIAM IS SUCH A BABY," Thomas complained.

"You cried when you were hurt, too. It is not wrong to want the comfort of your mother's arms about you." Nash pursed his lips, struggling not to follow Laura too closely in case he was needed. He did not like when they argued, especially when he had no defense. He had left her alone here too much, and she had needed him badly.

He waited until Laura got Liam on his feet and together, with Liam limping, they set off for Ravenswood again.

He put his hand on Thomas' shoulder and they started back to the manor together at a slower pace.

"Papa, can I ask you something?"

Nash nodded.

"Why is Mama talking about leaving?"

He inhaled. He'd wondered how long it would take for Thomas to ask about that. He was the most observant of the children due to his age. "Mama is angry with me because I did something very wrong. I hurt her feelings, and she is not done with giving me the set down I deserve."

"You never stay mad at us for so long when we misbehave."

"Well, I did something wrong for a lot longer than you ever have." He ruffled his son's hair.

"She went away, and we never saw her again," Thomas complained. "Didn't she love us anymore?"

"She had good reason to go, but listen to me: no matter how much Mama and I squabble, it has nothing to do with how she feels about you and your brother. She loves you both very much."

"And Isabelle, too?"

"And Isabelle."

"Do you love Isabelle?"

"Yes, as much as I do you and your brother."

Thomas chewed on his lip. "I like Belle very much."

"*Belle?*"

Thomas nodded and Nash laughed softly, liking the nickname for his daughter. "Well, I'm glad to hear you like her. She will need her big brother to protect her one day," Nash said and pulled his son into his side.

Things had changed for them all with Laura's return. Nash had never spoken of his feelings with his son, for one. But he liked the way things were now. He'd never been friends with his own father, but he hoped to be one for Thomas and Liam and Isabelle too,. Spending time with the children and Laura had given him a sense of belonging and purpose, quite different from how he felt about his brothers.

This was the way things should have been all along, or could be if Laura could ever overlook his shortcomings and ask to stay.

He sighed. There was still time to think of a way they might become friends, too.

When they reached Ravenswood, he sent Thomas off to find his mother and went in search of Algernon. He was not sure why he wanted to see his brother, though, other than to retrieve Isabelle. Algernon would just send Nash back to Laura immediately.

But he thought a little distance after their latest discussion might be in order.

Algernon was at a front window when Nash found him.

"Where's Isabelle?"

"With her mother already."

"Oh," he said disappointed to have been beaten to reach the child.

"Dear God, not now," Algernon complained.

"What are you looking at?" Nash peeked out at the drive, too, and gasped out loud.

Michael Sweet, a cousin they preferred to ignore, was standing on the drive beside his carriage and four.

"What the devil is he doing here?"

"He's the least of our concerns. Look who's with him," Algernon ordered, pointing to the carriage again, where a gray haired lady was being helped out of the carriage by servants. "What are we going to do about *her*?"

Lady Violet Eugenia Sweet, their father's youngest sister, had come home, and her sour expression was still locked in place.

"Dear God, Aunt Violet hasn't been here since we buried Mother. We're in for it," Nash answered, attempting to hide himself from being seen gaping out the window.

"It doesn't bode well to have the two of them together," Algernon complained, straightening his waistcoat and smoothing back his hair.

Nash frowned at his older brother. "You're not a boy anymore. You're the duke now. She cannot order you about like she did before."

"I will always be that unruly boy to her, and she will always tell me what I should do. Don't pretend she doesn't terrify you, too."

"Yes, but I'm just the spare," Nash replied, rushing to bring his clothing to order despite still being wet from his swim. Aunt Violet had terrified all the branches of the family at one time or another. She had looked down her long nose at them and criticized them for what she termed a disgraceful absence of moral character in the wider family.

However, in recent years, she had kept more or less to her own small estate, finally deeming them all unworthy of her company and opinion. But she wrote to everyone constantly, disparaging them for any gossip she heard. Father had preferred her far away from them all, and she'd sworn she preferred to be away from him, too

Father had believed his sister was a disgrace for failing to marry into a wealthy family. She'd disobliged him by not marrying at all.

The old girl walked with two canes now, instead of just the one he remembered her with when he was a boy, but she still managed the stairs at a sprightly pace, ignoring their cousin Michael's offer of assistance.

"The last I heard, Michael was in Derbyshire," Nash whispered. Keeping his voice low because even though Aunt Violet hadn't come inside yet, she had beyond-excellent hearing. She heard things everyone else seemed to miss.

"Our cousin has been traveling a great deal lately. His oldest sister complained about it to me at Amity's wedding breakfast," Algernon confided. "Come on. We must greet our unexpected guests with a smile."

At times, Nash did not always appreciate being included in greeting his brother's visitors. This was one of them. But he would have to speak with his aunt eventually, he supposed, so there was no point delaying the inevitable set down. Best to get the awkward encounter over and done with immediately.

They reached the entrance hall as the Ravenswood butler welcomed Aunt Violet back to the estate with transparent delight. The woman, nearly sixty years old now, looked him up and down and then nodded. "Home at last."

Algernon stepped forward. "Aunt Violet. A pleasure to have you visit us."

She looked him up and down, too, one brow raised. She scowled. "One does not visit one's home, Your Grace. One returns."

And then she did something extraordinary. She curtsied to her nephew, the new Duke of Ravenswood. Something Nash never thought to see in his lifetime. She'd little respect for their father when he'd held the title.

Algernon appeared stunned as well and glanced discreetly at Nash, before bowing in return.

Nash glanced at Michael, but he seemed to have no interest in the extraordinary exchange.

The last time Aunt Violet and Algernon had stood in the same room, she'd smacked him hard with her walking stick and told him to take himself away. They had argued about him not taking a wife. Algernon had refused to yield to her demands, just as he had their father's.

"Won't you come into the drawing room, Aunt," Algernon said.

"I prefer the sitting room. The ladies should be there by this hour, yes?"

"I... Ah," Algernon stuttered.

Aunt Violet stamped her canes on the parquetry floor. "Don't say you don't know everything that goes on in your own home?"

"Of course I do, but I, ah..." Algernon tried again, seemingly at a loss for words, and looked to Nash for rescue.

Aunt Violet began to laugh. "I see things have finally improved around here, if you are not sticking your nose into everyone's business like your father was prone to do." She turned away. "I trust my bedchamber has been prepared and tea already sent to the sitting room, Seymour. I wish to see everyone there in exactly twenty minutes."

She went on her way, not wanting or waiting for his reply or for anyone to guide her through the house she'd grown up in.

Nash glanced at Michael, who did not follow their aunt. "What is she doing here?"

"How should I know?" Michael protested. "Do you think I wanted to come to Ravenswood? Aunt Violet sent a letter demanding a carriage and my escort. I didn't know where we were headed until the morning we set out. She's up to something."

"Clearly you were meant to bear witness," Algernon mused.

"Actually, she said I could leave as soon as I care to," Michael said. "So I'm off. Best of luck with her."

"You can stay the night," Algernon offered, surprising Nash. They did not particularly care for Michael's company, though they liked him more than they did their horrible cousin George. "If you want to, that is."

Algernon moved away, issuing an order to the butler to make up another guest room, who'd rushed back to join them. The butler whispered in the duke's ear.

Nash kept a discreet eye on his cousin, who wasn't at all curious about the whispers, either.

Algernon sent the butler away. "It seems she's not come for a brief visit," he informed them. "She's come home to stay."

They both looked at Michael, who only shrugged. "That does explain the need for my carriage, when she had a perfectly good but older carriage of her own she could have used. The second carriage proved slower than mine and will probably arrive later tonight with the rest of her luggage and servants."

Algernon raked a hand through his hair. "Best gather everyone—and I mean everyone—in the sitting room. Get the surprise over and done with."

Michael raised a brow, but Nash ignored his cousin's expression. "I'll fetch my family now."

Nash hurried up the stairs, leaving Algernon to explain that Laura had returned with another child in her arms.

He discovered his family in Laura's bedchamber, Laura at her dressing-table mirror, fixing her hair. The boys watched her in obvious fascination. Isabelle was sitting on the floor between them, ignoring everything but the hem of her smock.

"I gather you saw the carriage on the drive?"

"Yes. They're ready to meet her," Laura promised, smoothing Liam's hair. The children had been quickly turned out into fresh clean clothes, hair brushed, and seemed excited.

Nash snatched up his daughter before she could put Laura's dress material into her mouth. He led his family downstairs to the morning room and the meeting with his aunt.

Laura snuck around him at the door and rushed across the room. She threw herself at the old lady's feet and, to his astonishment, the pair embraced. "How was your journey, Aunt Vi?"

"Tedious, my dear. That boy is not much for conversation, is he?"

Isabelle chortled and squirmed in his arms, and Nash struggled to hold her still.

Laura laughed softly. "He *is* as smart as he boasts though."

Nash's eyes narrowed with suspicion at Laura's praise for a cousin she'd had little to do with while they were together. How could she know cousin Michael so well?

"Yes, I suppose he must be. All he cared to talk about was investment and what I could do with my money and estate, as if I don't already know how the world works. I heard nary a word of a pursuit of a suitable wife or matches for his poor sisters."

"Give him time. He's still young," Laura urged, finally turning around to face the room. She beckoned their sons closer. "Thomas, Liam, this is your aunt, Lady Violet Sweet. Do you remember her at all?"

The boys shook their heads while the old lady looked them up and down. "A fine, healthy pair, despite growing up here under my brother's thumb." She lifted one of her canes and pointed it at each of them. Her gaze narrowed. "I see your father in you."

Nash tensed, ready to step between them, anticipating a blow from that cane that they could not possibly deserve.

Instead, her cane turned aside. "There is cake over there, children. One piece each. No gorging yourself like your father used to do."

Nash could feel his face heating. The boys headed straight to the table, each picking up a plate, taking one slice. They took small bites, and he was so impressed with their good manners. They kept their eyes on the old lady but seemed unafraid of her.

Aunt Violet nodded approvingly and turned her narrowed gaze on Nash. Then her dark eyes dipped to Isabelle, snuggled safely in his arms. "Bring the gel to me. Now."

Nash didn't want to give up his daughter to his aunt. She wriggled and gurgled as he held his ground.

Laura stood up, frowning at him. "Nash? Please?"

Reluctantly, and only because Laura asked, he brought his daughter closer to a woman who would likely criticize her, too.

Laura took Isabelle from him and dropped her immediately on the old woman's lap. The walking sticks fell aside as Aunt Violet embraced his little girl tightly. Her smile was blinding. "She's gown fat since I saw her last."

Nash's gaze flew to Laura in shock, but she wasn't looking at him. She knelt again beside the old lady and grinned. "She missed you, terribly, too," Laura promised with a playful laugh.

His aunt held Isabelle away from her, studying her, and her eyes danced with amusement. "So she should have. She's my favorite, and I simply must be hers."

Nash felt his legs grow weak. Laura had lived with Aunt Violet? They clearly knew each other well, and his aunt knew Isabelle enough to see the changes in her.

He sank into the nearest chair, mind spinning.

Laura had been with his family member at some point, but not one he'd ever thought to visit. No one willingly visited Aunt Violet...and that was how Laura had stayed hidden from him, and Father too, most likely. He could have easily found his wife and child, if he'd been on better terms with his aunt.

Algernon arrived, clearly taken aback by the sight of Isabelle in Aunt Violet's arms, as well. He recovered quickly and glanced at him.

"Take her back now," Aunt Violet said, dropping a kiss on the girl's cheek first before giving her up. "She's almost too heavy for me to hold for long."

Laura scooped her up, kissed Isabelle too, and

brought her back to him. She turned back to Aunt Violet. "Everything is arranged as you would wish."

Nash turned his gaze on his wife again and kept it there. Laura looked delighted by her own announcement. She had known their aunt was coming to Ravenswood and hadn't thought to warn them. Aunt Violet had once sworn she'd never return to Ravenswood without a good reason. Laura and Aunt Violet hadn't spent much time together, or had they?

Aunt Violet hadn't come for their father's funeral and had declined to attend cousin Amity's wedding breakfast. But she was here now, and clearly pleased to be so.

Laura might be the reason she'd returned, or perhaps was it Isabelle who drew her back home?

They could hide nothing from Aunt Violet if she stayed forever. She would learn about the debts Father had incurred and what they had done to save the estate. Nash would also have to contend with his aunts complaints when Laura finally left him, too.

"Damn," he whispered.

"Damned, indeed," Aunt Violet answered him, smiling. "Clearly you are still the smartest of my brother's offspring if you understand the situation you find yourself in now."

"We so missed your sunny disposition,

Aunt." Algernon rolled his eyes and bent to pick up the old lady's canes for her. "Your room is ready, should you like to retire and rest after your long journey."

"I will go when I am ready and not a moment sooner, boy. Where are the other ones? The new wife, particularly?"

"Stratford and Win are visiting Mr. Aston. I expect them back any day now."

"It will be good to see the old devil again. The only friend of your father's with any sense," she said, and then chuckled. "Although his eyesight has always left much to be desired." She glanced about the room again, lips pursed. "And the other one. The silly one. What's his name?"

"Jasper? I'm afraid you just missed him. He has left for London only this morning with the woman he will marry."

"And her name?"

"Sophie Radcliffe."

Aunt's eyes flickered between Laura and Nash. "The governess."

"Yes, they will be very good together, I'm sure," Laura promised her.

"I'll be the judge of that." Aunt Violet kept her narrowed gaze on Laura, and then her eyes widened in definite surprise. "Don't say it's another love match."

"Indeed, it is," Nash admitted.

Aunt Violet laughed, a rusty sound, as if she was unused to such things. "My brother must be restless in his grave. I must go out and pour salt on his wounds and increase the sting my return must be causing him."

Nash glanced outside and saw that it had begun to rain. "Perhaps when the weather improves," he suggested.

"It rained the day your mother died." Aunt Violet sniffed. "If only she were here to see you all. Now. Leave me."

Algernon stepped forward. "Aunt, let me help you up?"

"I do not approve of coddling at any age," she insisted as she snatched her canes from him. "But send the butler to attend me. We have much to discuss, he and I."

Although clearly puzzled by what their aunt and butler had to talk about, Algernon inclined his head and fled. Laura said a slow goodbye, clearly reluctant to leave the old woman so soon.

"Come to me tomorrow when you can and we'll talk again," Aunt Violet promised.

Nash was the last to exit the room. Him and Isabelle. He took the girl to his aunt.

Isabelle kicked her legs, clearly recognizing the old woman's face.

The woman laughed. "She's a gift, that girl."

He hugged Isabelle to him. "I quite agree."

The old lady scowled. "I meant your wife."

Nash did not answer that, but he agreed with her on that, as well. Laura had been a gift he'd not appreciated enough.

He took his leave of his aunt just as the butler arrived. Seymour hurried past him, and shut the door in Nash's face. Inside he heard his aunt begin issuing orders but whatever she was telling Seymour to do was none of his business anymore.

Nash strolled the house with Isabelle, talking to her and slowly headed toward the upper floors, mulling over why he was not angry over being duped by his own aunt. She had deliberately hidden Laura from him, and probably from his father, too. He soon decided he had no right at all to be angry about the latter.

Laura had been safe, protected by an older relative of his these last years. The new information and her diary entries made everything clear. Aunt Violet had always been fiercely devoted to the women of the family. She had been his mother's only friend.

He stopped in the hallway as he heard voices raised in anger. He pivoted toward the sound to find Algernon and Michael almost at each other's throats outside a guest bedroom.

He quickly got between them. "Enough."

"He started it," Michael complained, as if

they were still twelve and denied a seat at the older children's nursery table for supper.

"Don't make me finish it again," Algernon threatened. "He does not owe you anything, no matter what Father might have promised."

"This has nothing to do with your father."

There had never been much love between them and their cousins in the past. Father had pitted George, Michael, and Algernon against each other since birth. Michael, though, had grown up without brothers to back him up and had a chip on his shoulder a mile wide.

Isabelle whimpered, sensing the tension in the air, and he held her close, rocking her until she quieted. He pressed a kiss to her brow and studied his cousin over her head. "Uncle doesn't want to hurt cousin Michael, sweetheart, but Papa will if he has to. What seems to be the problem?"

"He claims you owe him," Algernon growled.

Nash frowned. "For what?"

"Looking at your face is enough," Michael countered.

Nash handed Isabelle to her uncle. Nash could fight his own battles. "Have you looked in the mirror lately, cousin? The older you get, the more like us you seem to become in your looks."

Michael's face colored. "I'm nothing like you lot."

"Looks, not character," Nash admitted. "I'm sure your father did a better job of raising you than ours did. Which means we know exactly how to deal with troublemakers. We have held back from teaching you that lesson many times in the past, but our patience has limits. My brother welcomed you to stay with no agenda. Can we not bury past disagreements and speak with civility for once?"

Michael reeled back on his heels, as if he'd not expected any attempt at reconciliation. But he recovered quickly. "I am still owed."

"For what, exactly?"

"For that child, for one. You wouldn't have her if not for me."

Nash's eyes narrowed on his cousin, noting the belligerence of his gaze and the return of a smirk. Behind him, Algernon gasped, taking the comment the wrong way, but Nash would not rise to the bait. There was no impropriety involved concerning Isabelle. "For how long exactly have you been her coachman?"

"Aunt Violet is a menace," Michael said, his face turning scarlet. "She's no right to order a grown man about."

"But we still do her bidding anyway," Nash replied. "You carried Laura away from Ravenswood."

"Not from here but I found her later. I took

her to Aunt Violet and she said...*demanded* I help her."

The later pieces of the puzzle of Laura's disappearance fell neatly into place. But how Laura left the estate so easily was still unanswered. Surely she had not walked off the estate. Vanishing without a trace and so well that Father never found her was quite the feat.

"You must have brought her to me in London, as well?" He paused until Michael finally nodded. And then the words he never expected to say to this particular cousin burst out. "Thank you. I *am* forever in your debt."

Michael nodded. "And I will collect."

"Whatever sum you require will be paid," Nash promised.

"I don't want money." Michael looked about. "What little you have left is not enough for the debt you owe me. Collection can wait until the time is right, and I'll be creative when I make my demands."

"Hmm, very well," Nash agreed. The safety of his wife and daughter were without price. He owed Michael everything for their safe return to his care. "I will look forward to hearing your demands at a later time, then."

"I'll be taking back the horse your wife borrowed when I leave as well."

Nash nodded.

Satisfied that he'd got the answer he wanted, Michael pivoted on his heel and strode into the guest room, slamming the door.

Algernon nudged him hard on the shoulder. "How could you do that? You just handed him everything on a silver platter without challenge. Who knows for how long his demand will hang over your head?"

"I owe him everything for protecting my wife from Father," Nash murmured. "Aunt Violet, too. It was something I should have done all along."

"I'm glad to hear it."

Nash glanced at Isabelle. His little girl was drowsing in Algernon's arms now. "You know, you ought to get one of these before you become too decrepit to hold them."

Algernon glanced down too and handed Isabelle back. "I've always wanted children."

"Then marry."

"The time is almost right," he said. "I promise."

CHAPTER SEVENTEEN

AFTER A HALF HOUR of futile searching, Laura found Nash in his chambers, rummaging around in drawers, by the sound of it. The door between their chambers was still shut, though. She'd have to open it to see what he was doing and try to explain about Aunt Violet.

She nodded to herself.

Now that Aunt Violet had come, it was time to unburden herself of her remaining secrets. Come clean about where she'd been living in hiding and make sure she had caused no lingering resentment toward his aged aunt.

Aunt Violet was not an easy person to love, but she was fiercely loyal to her family. Laura had confided in her about the problems with her life at Ravenswood and the duke once, and when Micheal Sweet had found her and taken her to

Aunt Violet she had received an invitation to stay with her instead.

Michael Sweet had been her unwilling participant but a speedy method of travel. He'd had no love for the late Duke of Ravenswood or Nash, and did the old lady's bidding without too much complaint because it meant he was thwarting them.

There had been enough strife in the family without Laura adding more to it.

She headed to Nash's door and put her hand on the latch. It was not locked again today and it swung open easily.

Nash was standing in his dressing closet, his shirtsleeves rolled up above his elbows. His coat had been tossed aside carelessly on the floor.

She took a few tentative steps in his direction and stopped, expecting him to hear her. He did not and continued searching. She looked around, saw the portrait of herself that was still hanging on the wall, and sighed. "Nash."

He did not answer. She took a few more steps toward him, curiosity getting the better of her about what he was looking for.

Beneath his hung clothes and about his feet was an untidy stack of journals. More accounting for the estate, she assumed. He had often had his head in a ledger when he should have been with her. Deciding she'd come at a bad time, she backed away.

Nash cursed. "I will just be one more moment. My apologies if I disturbed you." He turned about to look at her. His hair was untidy, his cravat missing and, despite all that, he looked very appealing today. "Did you want me?"

She did. Laura wet her lips, struck nearly dumb by an overwhelming desire to cross the room and pull that confounding man into her arms and kiss him. She dropped her gaze and controlled herself. "I could come back later if you're busy," she offered.

"No. Don't go." He straightened. "This might be of interest you."

"Oh," she said, puzzled. She had not come here to look at account ledgers. "I wanted to explain about your aunt."

"There's no need," he asked. "Her fondness for Isabelle tells me everything I need to know. Michael found you before I could. Michael found you and kept his mouth shut about it, and took you to her. Then later she brought you to London, where you expected to confront me but seduced me instead. He took you back to Aunt Violet, where Isabelle was eventually born."

Laura gulped. He knew everything.

"It's all right. I'm not angry. I had been worried you were all alone. Now, there is something I want to show you."

He returned to the dressing closet, bent, and picked up a stack of journals from the floor. He dumped them all on his bed and spread them out. "I want you to have these."

"I've no interest in the reading the Ravenswood estate ledgers."

"They are nothing of the sort. Look, Laura. Please," he whispered.

She moved to the bed, slightly distracted by its size because it was larger than her own. Nash followed and stood behind her.

"Where should I start?"

He reached around her and flipped open one book after another. She saw only a blank front page at first, and she turned the page of the closest book.

She gasped. "Thomas." The simple drawing was unmistakable. Someone had drawn her son.

"Yes, and this one is Liam's first volume."

Laura blinked. "Volumes?"

"I first started drawing the children soon after they were born, at night and anytime I was away from memory. I continue to this day. There are a lot of them sleeping."

"You did them all?" She took in the journals. At least a dozen were spread across the bed. "I did not know you could draw."

"No one does. My father did not approve of artists," he answered. "We had to hide Stratford's hobby for a long time. It has been my secret joy to draw our sons these past years, and now I can draw our daughter, too."

He drew another journal close, and it was easy to see it was brand-new. There was just one drawing of Isabelle, but it was so skillfully done her breath caught.

She stared at him. "Your brothers really don't know?"

"Not even Algernon."

"Why are you telling me?"

"Because you are their mother. You missed so much of the boys' lives because I drove you away. You should have these in place of the time that was stolen from you, and perhaps it will help you feel more connected to their pasts. You left a similar gift on my pillow the other day. Thank you for that."

Her hands trembled over the pages, and she longed to rush away with them and devour the contents all at once. Yet, these were Nash's memories, too. A product of his own hand. His secret joy was not hers to take away from him. "I cannot keep them, but I should like to look at them for a while."

There was a pause. "I drew you, too."

Laura stilled, eyes flicking to the sketch of her on the wall. "When?"

"All the time. They…" He inhaled. "They made me feel less lonely without you."

Laura could feel her body sway toward him, instinctively seeking to appease her own loneliness and comfort him. Yet what good would it do to tell him she'd felt the same?

Nash's hand settled on her upper arm. "You have no idea how great the void you left behind."

She closed her eyes. Damn him. He was reading her mind. She'd always felt his absence.

Nash's fingers closed over her other arm, and she was pulled back slightly toward him.

Laura trembled. Afraid of him, of herself, and what might happen next. "We were all wrong for each other."

"Yes, perhaps we were then. But never at night. At night, we were perfectly matched in all things that I thought were important for us."

She exhaled, eyes fluttering closed as she remembered how close they had been in her bed. "It was almost enough."

"We could be that way again," he offered in a whisper. "I have thought of you every day and night. Being this close to you, knowing you don't want me anymore, is utter torture. I can't resist wishing I could be different enough that you might want me again."

But Nash *was* different. The old Nash would never have voiced his wants out loud. He'd never once spoken of his feelings and desires to her before. She'd never been his confidant or known his secrets.

And now she did, and she could not fight how good that felt.

Oh, she'd always known what they had been in her bed when they were together. The connection, an onslaught of sexual gratification for both of them, had been exquisite.

But this new Nash was nearly a stranger to her. His wants at night might be the same, but during the day, now, she didn't dare assume anything at all about him.

She turned to face him, and Nash continued to hold her loosely before him. Waiting for her to decide if they would scratch the itch of lust together and become lovers once more.

She ought not to.

It was daytime and he'd see the damage done to her skin. The scars she'd never be able to hide were humiliating.

She'd best leave that only connection between them severed forever.

But her need for him was strong. She'd had this man. She knew his body, and he knew hers. There were many reasons not to give in and just one to say yes to him.

She had given him her heart and trust the day he'd proposed. She had trembled whenever he'd smiled her way and worse when she awaited him in her bed at night.

She still trembled whenever he was near. She was weak, and afraid, but he was so very familiar. He'd asked to see her scars already.

There was no one but Nash she'd ever show them to.

Her *husband*.

And he was right there, begging for a second chance. He was trying to change for her.

Couldn't she at least try as well?

She opened her eyes and looked up at her husband. "We cannot be what we were to each other again."

Nash blinked and dropped his gaze, but not before she caught a look of acute disappointment flicker over his face. "Forgive me, I—"

"Things must continue to change between us or we will die...and this time it will be forever."

His gaze snapped to hers.

"I will not be used and discarded when the sun rises," she told him.

"I never discarded you. I set you aside," he admitted. "I was very wrong to do that."

"Yes, you were. Now prove that you remember me this time," she whispered.

He grinned and was suddenly upon her, his

arms tight bands around her ribs. She sought his lips and found them willing and hungry for the kisses they had both missed.

Her gown and slippers disappeared faster than she dreamed was possible. With one sweep of his hand, the journals containing his precious drawings crashed to the floor. Nash placed her gently in the center of his bed, and she lay down —only to see a mirror image of herself above and the scars on her arms.

Nash had not noticed them yet and crawled over her on hands and knees and his lips went to her neck, nibbling and feasting in the way he used to do.

She couldn't take her eyes off them in the mirror above. Watching herself being made love to was strange, and she languidly put her arm about his neck and pulled him down for kisses from her lips.

Nash turned suddenly, glancing up at the mirror. "I'll have to draw this later." He laughed softly and reached for the waistband of his breeches. He shoved them down, baring his bottom.

She slid her hands down, touching his bottom the way she used to when they made love. Nash shuddered and groaned and flexed his hips against her. His erection butted into her belly, hard already, but he made no move to do more than that. Immediate copulation had never been his way. Not even the night they'd made Isabelle had been an entirely rushed affair.

They rolled around together on his bed, moaning and touching. Relearning each other's shape.

But it was different. She was waiting for his reaction.

It was daylight, and with that mirror hanging overhead, she saw everything she hated about herself.

Nash noticed her distraction and frowned at her. "Laura?"

Her gaze lowered to her right arm where the scarring was impossible to miss.

Nash froze above her. "The devil…"

"They took a long time to heal," she said rubbing her hand over them to hide them briefly.

Nash grasped her arm and pushed her other hand away gently. "These are deep. Too deep and too many."

"Yes, I know."

"The work of a butcher," he said, his thumb sliding back and forth over each one. He lifted her arm higher to study them and then noticed the other scar and grabbed her left arm. "This one is different."

"Yes. The work of a more impatient hand at work I believe," she murmured.

He glanced at her. "No physician would have cut so deep for any normal bleeding."

Her breath rushed out of her. "Yes, I know. The last morning here, I woke confused, with a pounding head and throbbing arm and to find a servant frantically pressing a cloth over the new bloody wound. There was a knife in my hand that I had no memory of seeing before. I had taken supper in my chambers the night before and I believe something was slipped into my food so I would sleep through what was done to me."

Nash sat back on his heels, his face turning white. "My God."

She nodded, relieved by his reaction. "I never saw who cut me, but I'm told the duke returned late in the afternoon the day before, only to hurry away very early the next morning. He spoke loudly of his concern for my recent behavior and ill health. He mentioned places where troubled women could be sent. One maid came to check on me because I had slept late that day. I believe she was meant to assume I had tried to hurt myself and was therefore a danger to the boys. She treated my wounds and offered to help me escape the duke without him, or anyone, learning about it. Even you."

"Laura, I..."

"It wasn't you," she said rising to sit up. She

touched his shoulder. "There wasn't anything you could have done."

"Had I known his true intentions I would have taken you away from here. I swear I would have. I am so sorry."

She put her finger over his lips. "Don't apologize for him again."

"What can I do then to make it up to you?"

"Help me the only way you can. Kiss me and make me feel safe again."

Nash nodded, removed his waistcoat and shirt, kicking off his lower garments, but she could sense his mood had changed. Hers had too but she needed him. She wanted to feel desirable still, too.

Nash was a deliciously muscular beast of a man she discovered. A perfect distraction from her troubled thoughts. The clothes he wore hid the strength of him, but the dark had not. Now confronted by the beauty of his body, her breath caught in wonder.

He dropped back over her, keeping most of his weight on his own hands. But his naked body brushed hers and she watched him move, reflected in the mirror above. The muscles of his back flexing were utterly fascinating and she ran her hands over his skin. Up and down and all over, making Nash moan.

Laura shifted to widen her legs, willing him

to hurry but she should have known it wouldn't be so easy.

His palm settled over her sex, startling her as the action always had. She could see now that it was a move of pure possessiveness on his part. She heard it in the sharp intake of his breath, saw it now in the darkening of his eyes.

Her body reveled in being near him again, and she squirmed as her sex clenched in anticipation for what was to come.

Fingers suddenly parted her drawers, seeking her slit. When he parted her lower lips and found her clit, Laura's back arched off the bed and a wail of gratitude escaped her.

"I never could get enough of that sound," he whispered. "Make it again."

"Nash," she chided, although she was amused by his demand.

His weight left her, and she opened her eyes to look at him. "That's better. Look up at what we do to each other."

His fingers moved against her clit and when she looked down, she saw the length of him, bobbing hard and untended.

She wet her lips.

In the dark of her bed, she had held him, stroked him and thrilled in making Nash moan. But it was so different in the daylight. She met his gaze, uncertain again. In the light of day, it was not just about appeasing lust. It was more.

So much more carnal than any nighttime coupling had ever been. She could see his excitement, and he could see hers.

A bead of semen hovered on the tip of his cock. She'd tasted Nash with her own mouth many times, but never seen his face while she did so.

She wanted to watch him for once.

Fingers trembling, she reached for his length and took him in hand.

Nash rocked into her touch, lips parting on a groan as the silky-smooth skin of his cock slid across her palm once more.

She watched his face, his body tense, his chest heaving as she stroked him harder, faster, saw him clench his jaw to hold back a groan, an oath or plea for more. He struggled to control his lust, and Laura grinned at the discovery. He was not alone in that. Laura was feeling quite wild.

She rose and took the head of his cock into her mouth.

A curse left Nash's lips, and suddenly they were lying side by side, heads in opposite directions. Nash parted her thighs and put his head between her legs.

The first lash of his tongue across her sex

made her cry out. It had been so long, and Nash was so good with his tongue.

He feasted on her sex, thrumming her clit, penetrating her sex with his tongue and sometimes his fingers. She squirmed against him, even as she sucked his cock down her throat. She was hungry for this. For him. For a chance to feel this good again.

Nash dipped his fingers deep into her, and she nearly shrieked for the forgotten joy of that too.

Yes, she was as wicked as Nash. She retaliated by tugging on his balls, and when he stopped groaning from that pleasure and pain, she took him into her mouth again.

Nash stilled suddenly, removed his head from between his legs. "Laura," he whispered. "Laura, look up."

With a little difficulty, she did.

What she saw nearly made her climax. Nash fingering her, teasing her toward a climax she so desperately longed for.

His hard cock was flushed with blood and poised against her parted lips. She pushed down, ramming herself onto his fingers. Nash resumed his feast at her sex while she panted and moaned. Laura watched them fondle each other until she could bear no more.

She climaxed, impaled on Nash's fingers, letting go of all the lust they'd built in such a short time with a loud wail.

"I can't stop," Nash warned, just as he jerked and overflowed her mouth with his seed. She swallowed quickly, but then he was there, kissing her to swallow up some of the excess that escaped her mouth.

They continued kissing for a moment, then Laura turned onto her back, panting hard.

Staring up at themselves, lying sated side by side, was different too. Nash reached for her hand and gripped it tightly, the way he always had in the dark.

It was confronting to see the aftermath of their intimacy at last. Her emotions were raw and clear on her face. The darkness had hidden them from him before, and his from her. Nash looked happy.

She wet her lips and gulped. "When did you get the mirror?"

Nash turned onto his side, lying so he faced her. "It's always been there."

"Has it?"

"But the view is better with you in it with me."

"Why did we not...sleep together here?"

"I don't know. At first, I suppose I thought you'd think me lewd or something. We were young, and I wished you to think well of me.

Then later, I realized the mirror was hardly needed for excitement when we were in bed together. You aroused me just by breathing."

Some response was required for such a flattering admission. She saw Nash's hand lying over hers in the mirror. Strong, possessive, familiar. She squeezed his fingers. "I like seeing you naked in the mirror."

She saw Nash smile. "I enjoy seeing you anywhere near me."

He rolled onto his back and closed his eyes.

Laura swallowed the hard lump in her throat. Nash would not be seeing her here again unless they changed their minds about a divorce.

He hadn't said he wanted that, and she couldn't be the first to suggest it, either. She had her pride.

Nash's breathing turned even and deep, and she freed her hand. When she was certain he slept deeply enough, Laura crept off the bed and left him there to wake up alone. She took some of his journals with her to pore over though.

CHAPTER EIGHTEEN

"SO, you see, this is a prime opportunity to turn a profit with little risk," Michael finished, after detailing an investment scheme that had definite possibilities. His current interest was in shipping, and the profits to be made close to home, and he'd sought Nash's opinion for once.

But frankly, Nash wished his cousin might have waited until tomorrow to bring up the matter. He was not in the right frame of mind to talk of cargo and yields with anyone.

Nash had made love to his wife again.

They had made love.

In the middle of the day, and it had been glorious.

The last thing he wanted to do now was discuss investments with a smug and previously hostile relative.

Nash would rather think about things within his control.

He was certain he had turned a corner in his marriage. Not just turned a corner, but hopefully reversed course entirely.

He wanted more days with Laura. Needed them, and her—even if they fought.

He would have them if only his cousin would go away or bother someone else with his grand ideas.

Michael pushed some papers at him. "So, what do you really think? Would you invest in such a venture if you had funds to spare?"

Nash pursed his lips, unwilling to admit out loud that he'd struggled to keep his mind on the conversation. It would cause an argument, and Michael appeared to be trying to mend fences by asking for his advice.

Laura had always had a distracting effect on him. Father had noticed and chided him for not listening so many times he'd lost count.

But Father was gone, and he answered to no one anymore. Except for Laura. "I think it is something you should definitely explore."

Michael regarded him for a long moment. "I thought, since you're familiar with it now, that you might like to ask your brother his opinion, and perhaps—"

"Unfortunately, I'm expected elsewhere soon," he blurted. "But do approach Algernon and seek his opinion, by all means."

"Yes, but—"

"Have you discussed the matter with him at all yet?"

"Not exactly. I came to you first because you handled many investments for the old duke and—"

"It was always Father's decision where he invested his money, and it is Algernon's decision now," he told his cousin, and then stood, impatient to escape. "He might be interested enough to join you, but that is for him to decide. Excuse me."

He took his leave of his cousin quickly. He'd not seen Laura enough today. She'd left him sleeping in his bed after they'd made love and he thought he knew why.

She hadn't wanted him to see those horrible scars again, or discuss father's secret plan for her demise. He'd closed his eyes only for a moment but had not expected to fall asleep. But his first release since the last time they'd made love had been spectacular. So many of his doubts had been erased that he could finally relax.

The scars did not change how he felt about Laura, except increase his devotion to her well-being in the future.

He hurried past Algernon in the hall and it was difficult to not warn him that their cousin had an idea he couldn't resist talking about.

Once upon a time, he might have handled the matter for him, deferred the conversation entirely until another day. But as the duke continued to point out, Nash had more important concerns than the ducal estate.

The only thing vital to him now was to settle the matter of his marriage continuing, if it wasn't already saved.

Today had been a first step. Large but the first of many, he hoped. Acknowledging their attraction would go a long way toward easing the tension between them. Unsatisfied lust clouded the issues of what went wrong in their marriage. Their sex life was the only thing that had satisfied either of them. That and the children.

And now there were three. Three small, adorable beings who depended on him to make their world happier. He had failed them all for some time. He'd allowed them to be set to one side as well.

No more.

He continued on, upstairs to the nursery. Laura was sitting with Isabelle on her lap, crooning a lullaby to her. Thomas and Liam were lying on the floor nearby listening, heads on pillows and looking very sleepy.

It was a scene he always wanted to remember.

Nash backed from the room quietly, hurried to his own chamber and found a new journal. He wanted to capture that moment of his family being together. Capture it and keep it as a reminder of all that they should have always been.

A family that loved each other with their whole hearts.

He crept back into the room to find Laura still, Isabelle cradled close to her chest and sleeping. Thomas and Liam had closed their eyes while he was gone.

Nash slid to the floor, opened his sketchbook and began drawing.

Laura's lips twitched. "I seem to recall now you scratching away in your journal before. I always thought you were working on some scheme for your father."

"So did he. I always showed him a page with small calculations if he asked what I was doing," he whispered.

"Why did you never want anyone to see your drawings before today?"

He drew the curve of Laura's arm around their sleeping daughter. "I did not think highly of them."

"But you do now?"

"Not really," he grinned. "I still think they

would make others laugh. Stratford is a much better artist. He could practice more."

She frowned. "What I have seen so far is very good, very accurate."

Praise had been so rare in his life. Hearing Laura speak well of his work made his cheeks heat. "Thank you."

He continued sketching, even when Laura stood to put Isabelle into her bed. He would add to the image over the coming days until he was satisfied it was drawn exactly right. Laura moved away to a window, watching him work. "I used to see you out there, sitting with your journal and ignoring us up here."

"I went out there to get away from prying eyes."

"Your father's."

"And my brothers'. They took up a lot of my time then."

"And they do still. How was Michael?"

"Tedious. He wanted me to put in a good word for him, but I've developed more exciting interests."

Laura glanced down at her fingers. The ring he'd placed on her hand so many years ago was still missing. She lifted her gaze and studied him in return. Nash closed the book and gave her his full attention. He would put her first as often as he could now.

The heat of desire was still there between them as they stared at each other, barely tempered by the passage of a few hours since they'd made love.

As a new husband, he'd been unsettled by how much he desired this woman. Now, after growing older and being without her for so long, he felt finally at peace with his lust.

There was nothing wrong with wanting one's wife, not when she wanted you as much.

Father had always claimed wives had little use besides procreation. Nash pitied the life his mother must have endured with such a bitterly cold and controlling man. A man he'd almost become.

He got to his feet slowly and went to stand before Laura. If he wanted her, he had to continue to share his innermost thoughts. "This morning was good."

"Yes."

He pursed his lips. "I enjoyed seeing you in my room."

"Did you?"

He nodded quickly. "I wondered if you would agree to a change in our arrangement."

"What sort of change?"

"A pleasurable one, I promise."

Her eyes widened.

"I would like us to sleep in the same bed again," he whispered.

She at least considered his request, but then shook her head. "No. This morning was all the risk I am willing to take."

He was prepared for her immediate refusal.

"We would limit our activities to prevent conception," he offered. Laura had been very firm about not wanting to have more of his children already. Her desire to curtail certain aspects of lovemaking was understandable, but not enough to deter him from asking for what they *could* share. "I can find satisfaction without penetration. So can you. My lips, tongue, and fingers are at your disposal, always."

She glanced over his shoulder at their sleeping offspring, but he could tell she was becoming excited by his blunt talk. The rapid rise and fall of her breasts excited him, too. He inched closer, lowering his voice. "I have not spent enough time worshiping your body, and I could happily spend an eternity between your legs."

Laura's breath caught, and she turned to gaze up at him, eyes wide with shock and hunger.

The children were fast asleep, but there was no maid due to come to take over until late in the evening. He could not wait that long, and he suspected she might not like to, either. He held out his hand to Laura. She swayed into him and he steered her out of the room. They required a little privacy to scratch this itch.

There was a small closet across the hallway, and knowing time was short, he led her into it. It was the perfect place for a swift and satisfying tryst.

He got her into the room, shut the door, and bent his head. He kissed her hard and fast, then used his thumbs to ease her gown from her shoulders.

Once her breasts were bared, he wasted no time kissing them. He tasted milk when he suckled too hard and lapped it up quickly. However, he knew better than to get carried away there. Her breasts were likely still Isabelle's, though he wasn't entirely sure about that.

He passed Laura his handkerchief to catch any drips as he lowered to his knees before lifting her skirts high. Laura had always enjoyed being kissed between her legs, and she was not wearing the white drawers she'd worn that morning.

He took his time teasing her to begin with, dropping kisses up her bare thighs and inhaling the scent of fresh arousal.

But he knew that their time alone would be severely limited until tonight. The children should never wake to find themselves alone in the nursery, nor could he and Laura allow a maid to discover them, either.

He parted her thighs and tilted her hips toward his face. At the first brush of his lips against her sex, her legs trembled.

He smiled, remembering all the times he'd made love to her in her bed. The memory of those often frantic exchanges made him look up to see her expression.

Laura watched him, and then she curled her hand around his skull. She guided him to put his mouth back between her spread thighs. She rose on her toes at the first touch of his tongue, but soon settled on his face, demanding satisfaction he was only too happy to provide.

He brought his fingers to work inside her sex, too. She was wet and stifling her moans to everything he did. He hastened his actions, determined to make her climax.

And she did, her hand clamped over her lips and her hips jerking against his face, her juices on his tongue. There was no better flavor in the world than Laura.

Sweet, sweet Laura.

He was not sure he deserved this second chance, but by God, he would make this work. He could give her exactly what she needed from him.

He sat back on his heels, aware of the throb of his cock, and pulled down her skirts and straightened them again.

He watched Laura as she composed herself.

She seemed uncertain of what to do next, so he stood and pressed a kiss to her cheek. "I'll take a peek at the children to make sure they're still asleep. Join me when you can."

He left her there, grinning to himself. Things were finally going in the direction he wanted with his wife.

But as he crossed the hall, he heard two thumps to his right.

He turned slowly and discovered Aunt Violet had made it up to the nursery wing, with the butler following close behind, too. Dear God, he'd been caught misbehaving by the old maid of the family and their oldest employee, too. "Can I help you, Aunt Violet?"

"I wish to speak with your wife and children."

He glanced around, stalling for time. "The children are asleep and Laura has just run downstairs to fetch a shawl, but will be back in a moment. Perhaps you might like to wait in the nursery until she comes back. Or I can bring them to you..."

"After the effort of getting up here, I will wait in the nursery," Aunt Violet said, drawing closer.

Nash moved to stand across the doorway where he'd left Laura to compose herself.

Aunt Violet's gaze flickered to the door behind his back, and then she smirked. "Don't rush on my account, my dear girl," she called out, before she and the butler disappeared inside the nursery room, leaving him stunned.

He let out a shaky breath, and then the door behind him slowly creaked open. Laura emerged, looking completely flustered.

"She knew you were in there and what we'd been doing," he whispered to her, and then winced. "If she'd heard anything, she hid her shock well."

Laura pressed her hands to her cheeks. "She's not as prudish as you might imagine about such things, but I certainly still am."

"We're married so there's nothing wrong in what we do together. However, she should be more shocked, since Aunt Violet never married," he argued.

"Only because your family would never have approved of her choice. She once told me your father tried to match her with a friend of his. She escaped him, like I did, and a very disagreeable match it must have been indeed."

Nash groaned under his breath. "Do you know who the fellow she really wanted might have been?"

Laura shook her head. "She never said his name to me. Well, I'd best see what she wants now."

Nash dropped his gaze to his wife's lips until she bit one. He grinned and met her gaze. "Do you want me to keep you company?"

"I think I can manage your aunt without you for a while. In fact, it might be best if I dine with your aunt tonight. Do you mind?"

"I don't mind, but I will miss your company. Will the children dine with you or me?"

"With me. Aunt Violet wants to get to know the boys and she has missed Isabelle dreadfully."

"Well, if you need me, I'll be around...or you'll find me tucked into my bed by ten o'clock waiting for you." He caressed her cheek with the back of his fingers. "If there is anything more you want from me before that, just send for me?"

Her lips twitched. "I'll consider it."

"Until later, then," he agreed, but he did not hold out much hope that he wouldn't be sleeping alone again tonight. Laura was skittish about him.

She slipped into the nursery and shut the door.

Nash turned for the stairs and descended the three levels to the ground floor. It really was inconvenient to trudge up and down so many stairs just to see the children. And for Laura, and even Aunt Violet, it was especially hard with their long skirts on the steeper flight to the nursery.

Nash headed for the abandoned apartment again.

Nothing had changed since his last visit, and he was struck again by how much easier life would be if his family moved down here. There was but one flight of steps down to the kitchens for the servants, a half flight out to the grounds. He would not worry about Laura carrying Isabelle up and down steep stairs. They would have space to be together apart from the duke and his visitors, and yet remain part of the family home.

He could never give Laura back her old family estate or the life she'd enjoyed there. But he could give her this and hope that went some way toward increasing the appeal of staying married to him. She would have her own space, her own home inside Ravenswood.

That had to be better than their current arrangement, surely.

A footstep sounded behind him, and he turned to see the butler at the door. "Can I be of any assistance, Lord Nash?"

"Seymour, you're just the man I need right now," he promised. "Have you got a few servants going spare?"

"I can make them available, of course."

"Good, because I want this apartment to have a thorough dusting—but it needs to be done in one night as a surprise for my wife."

The butler raised a brow but nodded. "I'm

sure more than a few would be willing to lose a couple of hours of rest for such a worthy cause."

Nash rubbed his hands together and went to the rotting drapes and pulled them down himself, covering himself and the spluttering butler in a cloud of dust.

"HELLO, IS ANYONE HERE?" Laura called, stepping into an unfamiliar room with her sons by her side. She was annoyed by this summons. She was also annoyed with Nash for not being in his room last night when he'd promised to be there by ten. She had gone to bed alone and disappointed.

She glanced around, expecting the duke.

But Algernon was not here.

Nash burst out of a distant chamber with a dirty cloth in his hand and rushed toward her. "Come in, come in," he called. He spread his arms. "What do you think?"

She glanced around again. The chamber was clean but had an unloved air about it. "It's a room."

"One of many in this apartment. Did I ever mention that a great uncle of mine lived at

Ravenswood? He kept to himself in here. Occupying this set of rooms apart from everyone."

"I vaguely remember something about someone. He was before my time here."

"The rooms were abandoned ever since, but look at them now." Nash set his dust cloth aside.

She walked around, realizing the abandoned room had only recently been cleaned, and Nash had taken some part in cleaning it, too, judging by the state of his clothes and satisfied smile.

Beyond this chamber were several connecting rooms, all of good size and filled with light, since there were no curtains hanging at the windows. And at the end of the chamber, there was even a separate door to the east gardens that she'd known no one to use before. "Why are you showing me this?"

"Because I would like to move us here today, with your permission," Nash said quietly, but it was obvious that he was excited about the idea as he pointed around them. "The children will share the end room at first, and when Isabelle is old enough, she will have the one beside it. This larger room will be the family sitting room, with books and comfortable chairs and a round table near the window that's big enough for us all to sit together at for meals." He walked past her and pushed open two sliding doors to reveal a large chamber. "This would be your room, whenever you are here."

She gaped at the huge space. There was nearly enough room for two beds, for a husband and wife and all of their belongings as well. "Where will you sleep?"

"I shall bed down in a smaller room farther down the hall." He drew closer. "This way, you will not have to climb those steep stairs to the nursery to see the children, or risk a fall when you carry Isabelle up and down. She wriggles a lot. And Aunt Violet can more easily visit you and the children here. But most important of all, the children would always have us close by."

She sniffed, overwhelmed by the change he planned to make for the family, and had considered for her future visits, too.

"I know. Too little, too late most likely, but..." Nash whispered.

She wrung her hands, conflicted about how to think of all he'd done. "And your brother has agreed to this?"

"Not exactly. I have not asked his permission to move because it is *our* home, too. I want to do this for you. For us all."

"I would have loved to live here before, so close to the children," she whispered.

"Then it's settled." He walked away, pulled on the bell four times, and then faced her again.

"I've got every servant poised to come and help with the transition."

Laura nodded, wildly impressed with Nash's decision to live closer to the children in the future. The distance to the nursery had always bothered her, and so had the stairs. "Living in an apartment inside Ravenswood will feel like a proper home for them."

"It is a long overdue change. I admit I considered it before, but Father would not hear of his grandchildren sleeping anywhere but the nursery."

She nodded, unsurprised by that.

The first servant arrived, and then more, all carrying something. She recognized nursery furniture and possessions belonging to the children.

Nash drew close again. "Tell them where you want everything to go, and it will be done exactly the way you want this time."

He hurried out, and she was left to direct the servants on her own. It took hours, all told, to move the children into their room, and then for her possessions to be brought down and put away in her new bedchamber.

Nash was no help at all, which she actually loved. He only carried in his personal items, papers and journals, storing them down the hall somewhere.

When the boys' room was ready first, they

bounced around, looking out the window and enjoying their new space. As soon as Isabelle's cot was made, she put her daughter inside for a sleep.

But the work carried on well into the afternoon, until finally the servants' footsteps faded away and the door remained closed behind them.

Nash appeared at the doorway to her new room and smiled. "Tea?"

"I'll ring for it," he promised.

She followed him out to the family room.

The apartment now boasted a warmth it had formerly lacked. She liked the large seating area particularly, and the cozy atmosphere she'd made with a rug on the floor, pillows on chairs, and being able to see the children just by lifting her eyes or turning her head.

She wandered down the hall to the room Nash was planning to occupy. It was quite small for him, almost a closet, and cramped with a narrow bed and just a chair beside it to hold his journals.

She glanced back at him. "Are you sure about this?"

"It only needs to be big enough for me to sleep in." He tipped his head. "I'll spend most of my time in the larger room with everyone."

Isabelle called to her, but Nash was quick on his feet and reached their daughter before she could call out again. She glanced back into his room once more and realized Nash was making sacrifices for *her*. By rights, as the current heir to the Ravenswood title, he should have commandeered the largest room.

But he had given that honor to Laura and had not assumed he would share her bed. And he'd made sure he would always be close to his children, and her, until she went away.

She drew back, heart pinching with regret and wishing Nash could have been this man all along. She strolled back into the sitting room and found him walking around the large space with Isabelle held aloft and giggling.

"I think she likes it better here."

"Careful. Jasper did that with Isabelle, and she cast up her accounts over him," she warned quickly.

Nash lowered her onto his hip, grinning. "But I know the trick to avoid that better than him. I know when Isabelle last ate, and I am safe."

Laura nodded. Nash did know his children better now. There at least had been a benefit to Algernon ordering them together. She knew now that Nash did love them all. He would care for them in her absence. They would never be forgotten or set aside ever again.

She allowed Nash to serve her tea when it came and sipped a perfectly made cup. There were her favorite biscuits and some fruit on a plate but she was not hungry. She sat back and watched her family settle into their new quarters that night with a heavy sigh. Their new home. A place where they could be together with little outside interference at last.

A servant knocked on the door, and Nash hurried to answer it.

Laura closed her eyes, expecting it to be another summons from Algernon. It was past time for their last talk. Tomorrow was day thirty, and her time here was at an end.

Nash returned, gave her a smile and sat back in his chair as if he planned to stay there awhile.

"Are we ignoring His Grace today?"

"We absolutely are. If he wants us, he'll have to find us. Eventually he will."

She laughed softly and wriggled in the unfamiliar chair, repositioning herself to a more comfortable angle.

Her family was scattered around her. Thomas and Liam seemed ready to fall asleep on a thick floor rug. Isabelle lay on the chaise before her, eyes fluttering closed.

Nash reached out a hand toward her.

She took it and squeezed. "We ought to send the children to their beds, but I am honestly too tired to stir myself."

"Then don't move," he whispered. "Just enjoy."

She was having trouble keeping her eyes open, though. "It has been a very long and eventful day," she agreed.

"It has indeed." Nash squeezed her fingers. "Are you happy?"

She closed her eyes. "Yes, as a matter of fact, I am."

Laura jumped the next moment and opened her eyes, but the room was cast in deep shadows where before it had been filled with light, and Nash was no longer holding her hand.

Her gaze turned to her husband, seated still at her side. Nash had fallen asleep too, no doubt lulled by the warmth of the room and their recent exertions, as she must have been.

She exhaled and sank back again, determined to wake herself up properly before she disturbed anyone else, and considered her future.

The last few days, she and Nash had settled into a routine that was not at all unpleasant. Spending time together alone, just the five of them at the end of the day, away from his brothers. Not even the arrival of unexpected guests had drawn him away for long.

And now they had this apartment to share for her final day at Ravenswood.

This was everything she had hoped for from her marriage in the beginning—a place of their own, the feeling of belonging and the security that should have come with that.

She had given Nash thirty more days of her life and had only one regret.

It was over now...or would be tomorrow.

Their togetherness had largely healed her hurt, but not all of her fears for the future. Leaving Nash, leaving her young family behind, would cause a new tear in her heart that she might never recover from.

Nash still talked about the divorce as if it would happen. But then...he had tried several times to discuss her plans for the future, and she hadn't wanted to. As time wore on, those nebulous plans of hers had lost their appeal entirely. As did walking away from a man who meant everything to her again.

She had not expected that to happen. Laura had imagined they would fight until the very last moment. But as she looked at him now, sleeping and untidy again, she finally understood that his behavior had never been deliberately cruel. They had married young, perhaps too young to understand how they affected each other's happiness.

Liam yawned loudly and Nash jumped, waking himself, but the other children slept on. He stretched, her great beastly husband, and sat up. He glanced at her and smiled warmly. "My apologies."

"None are needed."

His smile was hesitant. "It was a good day."

That smile of his twisted a knife in her heart. His uncertainty had become somehow endearing and made her content. He did not always know what he was doing, but he tried to pretend that he did.

Laura had done the same, and their matching uncertainty soothed her in a way she'd never felt before. "It was indeed a good day."

He seemed delighted to hear it and glanced at his pocket watch. "I'd best summon our supper, yes?"

"Yes. They will be hungry when they all awake."

Nash went to pull the bell, came back and ruffled Thomas' hair to wake him, and then lifted Isabelle up into his arms.

Isabelle resisted waking. Nash brought the girl close to her and his fingers lightly brushed across his daughter's rosy cheek. "Time to play again, angel," he murmured.

She wriggled to be let down and crawled across to Thomas, who hadn't yet sat up. She cuddled into his side, and Thomas smiled down at his little sister and talked to her.

Laura could feel sadness threaten to overwhelm her and hurried to stand. For want of something to do, she went to each of her children's beds and turned back the bedding for later that night, listening all the while for what went on behind her back. They would be all right without her. They would have each other.

"Will you read to us tonight, Mama?"

She turned. Thomas stood at the door, book in hand. It was the first time he'd asked her to do anything for him. She wiped away a tear that he'd reached out to her at last...just before she was to go. "Yes, Thomas, I would love to read to you."

Thomas rushed away again, going to his brother and whispering to him. Nash watched on, smiling to himself.

She hoped Nash would never again be the cold man she'd had to leave but she understood now why he'd been that way. He was more aware of the boys than she'd ever given him credit for, interested in them both. So gentle with Isabelle, too, almost as if he was afraid she'd break. It broke her heart all over again that in the beginning, he'd never shown this softer side around her because of his father.

He loved each of their children, and she was relieved that they would not have the same cold upbringing that he'd suffered through.

Laura approached him, and his smile grew.

"I never imagined we'd have another child, but I am glad for our daughter," Nash whispered.

"There is nothing I won't do to protect her and make sure she's always happy."

Laura nodded. Isabelle had claimed a place in her father's heart so very quickly indeed. He loved her and was not afraid to say so. Laura had never been so lucky. "Try not to spoil her too much."

His expression changed a little as he sighed. "I'll do my best, but I can't make promises about that."

She was glad that he would speak openly about his doubts to her now. But her eyes filled with tears as she looked at her family. How had she ever found the strength to leave them behind the first time? She was not sure she would survive a second separation from them without falling completely apart.

Her eyes burned with unshed tears, but they could not be stopped. Fearing she might sob aloud and alarm the children, she fled the entire apartment for some privacy in the dark garden.

Nash caught up with her, and to her surprise, pulled her immediately into his arms.

He held her tight and said nothing about her flight. But this time, she was grateful for his silence. She could not have answered him right then. Her emotions were too raw and choppy for coherent speech. Later, tomorrow, she would find the words she hoped to say to him before they discussed her going away at last.

When she was quiet, he kept his arms about her. "I will miss them," she whispered.

"I always do when I'm away. They are young, but they will always have each other to rely upon."

She nodded quickly, dashing away another tear. The boys were close, just like all Sweet siblings seemed to still be. "And now Isabelle has her brothers to watch over her."

"And me," Nash promised. "I imagine she will keep us on her toes when she's older."

"Yes, she will," Laura told him. "You are so good with her, Nash."

"Not as good as you."

He held out his free hand, and she took it, squeezed his fingers tight. She would miss Nash as well. More than she imagined possible.

He drew her hand to his chest and held it tight against him. "I'm glad you came back when you did. I'm glad we settled our differences."

She met his gaze in the twilight garden and fresh tears stung her eyes. "So am I," she promised in a whisper.

Nash wet his lips. "Laura, would you take a stroll with me in the gardens? If you're not too tired, that is."

Time alone with Nash now was precious. "I

would enjoy that very much, but what about the children?"

"Thomas and I have had a little talk about the responsibilities of being an older brother. He knows when we are not there, he is in charge of his siblings. Especially with Isabelle being so young. If he has any trouble, he will ring for a servant immediately, but I'm sure he'll be fine without us for a little while. Their supper is on the way, after all."

"Yes, I'm sure they will be fine for a little while."

Nash threaded her arm through his.

Nash sighed heavily and glanced up at the manor. He waved, and she realized the children were watching them from the windows of the new apartment. Laura waved too, and their little faces disappeared.

"Algernon has made it abundantly clear during this month that he no longer needs me. My brothers have their wives and their own lives to live."

"Your brothers will always need you," she said, stopping so she could still see her family's new abode in the fading light. It was only a matter of time before his family came around again. She hoped they would not come between Nash and the children, though.

"But *our* family needs me more than my

brothers do, and I will do my best not to disappoint you again. I promise you, our family is my first and only concern now."

Laura stared at the rising moon and believed he meant that now. Nash had changed these past weeks. She only wished his newfound dedication to his family had occurred much earlier and could have included her from the start. It made leaving Ravenswood easier, but also so much harder. "I'm glad for you. You are a good father to them. The very best," she whispered, before she burst into tears again.

Unfortunately, she couldn't seem to stop them this time. Suddenly, she was in Nash's arms again, and she clung to him for comfort—afraid that it might be the last embrace she ever received from him.

CHAPTER TWENTY

NASH HELD Laura as she sobbed without restraint, her faced burrowing against his cravat and her hands clawing at his chest.

He felt as rocky as she did. The idea of their parting ways tomorrow felt wrong. In the morning, they would speak with the duke together and give him their final answer to the problem of their marriage and divorce.

He knew what he would like to say. He'd known for some time.

The last month had been difficult. Difficult, but strangely, the best days of his life. He had spent every day examining his feelings for Laura and the children. Yes, they had bickered in the beginning, struggling to understand each other and attach blame. They had also tried to ignore each other's appeal, but to no avail.

But those struggles and even the embarrassing discussions seated before the ducal desk with that ridiculous hourglass keeping them in their seats had finally cleared the air between them.

He knew now what was missing from his life. The truth.

He loved his wife. He had loved her from the very beginning. He'd just never told her so in words.

He'd foolishly imagined that his need for her at night, the passion they shared, had made such a discussion unnecessary.

The last week particularly had been the most satisfying, both in and out of bed, and he never wanted it to end. But it would soon end, and permanently, because Laura hadn't even hinted she had changed her mind.

Nash had previously decided to divorce Laura before he really knew how vital she was to his happiness. Laura had decided even earlier that she would be happier without him.

Yet how could she cling to him now if he was still someone she despised?

He didn't want their marriage to be over anymore. He wanted more days like today, and to spend his nights knowing Laura was nearby. Being woken by their children and starting each new day together.

He was certain he would never find such

happiness with anyone else. His decision to re-marry without understanding his need for love had been foolish.

Now, he could not let Laura leave him without knowing the truth of his heart. He must make one last attempt to save himself from heartache, and perhaps he could save her the same as well.

"There is something I want to discuss with you, Laura. But I have been hesitant to bring it up out of fear of what you might say."

"What is it?"

He wet his lips. If he did not make his wishes known now, he would never have a chance again. Laura had not shared her plans for the future, and he was afraid he might never know them. He took a deep breath and bent down toward her a little. "I wondered if...if you might like to stay married to me?"

Laura drew in a sharp breath, stiffening in his arms, but she did not immediately reply.

"I know it is not what we agreed upon, and your answer will not affect your ability to visit the children, but my feelings concerning a divorce from you have reversed. I wondered if you might have reached a similar conclusion."

He swallowed the sudden lump in his throat as he waited for an answer that would yet again alter the course of his life.

But Laura pushed away from him and stalked off. Darkness descended over them as clouds snuffed out the brightness of the rising moon and his wife's figure, too. He hurried to catch up with her lest she slip away.

She only went as far as the end of the path though. Her shoulders hunched as she stood looking over the estate. "I did not expect...that is to say...," she began.

Laura did not say more. In the silence, he could not make out her mood. Was she shocked he'd dared make the suggestion? Was she repulsed by the idea of remaining his wife?

He rushed to explain himself. "If we stayed together, I promise we would not have the same marriage as before. The duke might still need me sometimes, and I might have to leave you and the children behind on the odd occasion. And we might still squabble and may even fall out with each other again and again. But you must know that whenever I was away from you in the past, I wished always to return as fast as I could."

He waited for her response, and thought he would wait all night and perhaps even for years until he heard he still had a chance to win her back.

But she said nothing, and his hope withered.

"Forgive me. I had hoped a change of mind

had come over both of us. You must think me foolish."

She turned. Tears streamed down Laura's cheeks unchecked. She ignored them and set her hand on her hips. "You're saying you want me to stay with you now?"

"I do." His pulse sped up. "Because this happiness, the contentment I feel, will go away when you do."

Her hands dropped to her sides, and she drew closer, staring up at him. "You once asked me why I married you?"

"You told me," he whispered, dreading what more she could say about her decision.

"I accepted you because I admired you from our first meeting," she answered. "From our first dance, I wanted no other man's arms around me. You made me believe you cared for me, and then, after the wedding, you disappeared from my life a little more each day that followed. Why else would I be so angry that you allowed your father to come between us? I waited for you every time you went away, until I could bear to wait no more."

"It is my eternal shame that I wasn't strong enough to stand up to my father, and that you suffered for it. I am *glad* he is dead and you are free of him."

"We are both free of him, Nash," she whispered. Her fingers settled on his waistcoat lightly. "There is nothing but our own poor decisions to keep us apart anymore. I am not without fault in this marriage. I should have tried harder to tell you what I felt. You are not solely to blame for the mess we made of it."

He captured her hands. "Yes, we each made mistakes, but there is still time to learn from them, isn't there?"

"Yes, we have all the time in the world now. But we will probably make more mistakes, as you pointed out," she warned. "The making up has been the best part of our reunion, though."

He exhaled in relief, because that was the answer he needed to hear. Her patience and forgiveness, even her anger, had made him a better husband. "Indeed, it has, but I don't want to fight with you anymore. I want to be your friend, and to have you as mine."

She took another step in his direction and removed her hands from his, sliding them up to his shoulders as she sighed. "I hear some friends will fight just for the fun of it so they can chase each other and make up."

"I could happily bear a future like that," he agreed, having trouble containing the smile her words inspired in him.

Laura's eyes danced with amusement, then softened. "I love you, Nash. I always did. But you were so distant so often, I doubted you *and* myself."

He pressed his head to hers. "And I worried too much about what others might say if they discovered how much I adored you, craved you, even before we were to wed. That is why I pushed for an expedient wedding. I feared I might lose you to someone else."

"There was no chance of that." Laura winced. "Did it pain you to think I might have accepted Algernon as my husband?"

It had. "It was the only time I was ever jealous of his grand future. Our fathers talked openly about what a splendid match it would be if you married him, and it infuriated me that no one imagined you'd say no to a future duke."

"I would have very easily." Her fingers teased into his hair. "I never found Algernon at all attractive. Not the way I do you."

"I always wanted you on my arm instead of his," he continued, smiling now about the distant memory of fear and worry over losing her. "Not speaking with him about things you would never tell me afterward."

"Algernon only spoke of your brothers, shocking me with tales of the family scandals, and of your reactions. I didn't want to embarrass you by repeating anything he might have said to me in confidence. You have such pride in your family. Algernon never sought to impress me. I thought he was trying to scare me away, but now I think it was all part of his plan to suggest who might suit me better. He spoke of you in glowing terms."

"He knew, without me saying a word, that I was smitten with you," Nash whispered, placing his lips against her temple and exhaling all the tension left in him.

"It was always you, Nash. You became the man of my dreams and my nights. But I need that man as my husband all the time."

Nash slid his hands beneath Laura's arms and hoisted her high into the air. "I'm here."

She shrieked in surprise, and he lowered her again.

Laura laid her head on his chest. "This was all I wanted, you know. To have you show me you wanted me for more than your heirs and my dowry."

"I was a fool."

"Yes, you were."

He turned her face up to his. "A fool as much in love with you as I ever was. Perhaps more."

They kissed, but then Laura groaned. "We had best tell the duke that there is no need for an interview tomorrow, or he will summon us," she whispered.

"He can try, but he already told me what our

decision would be. He can wait until tomorrow to learn he was right all along." He cupped her face. "I trust you will warn me if I stop paying you enough attention."

"I will, but I expect to be rewarded if I have to."

"I'll be lavish as I beg your forgiveness." Nash smiled and kissed her again.

"Excuse me, Papa?"

Nash glanced past Laura to see Thomas outside, holding Isabelle, with Liam standing just behind and watching their parents kiss in the dark.

Laura buried her face in his chest and laughed. "Caught again."

"This seems to be becoming a habit." He kept Laura close. "Yes, son?"

"Supper has arrived."

"Ah, yes. I will be there in a moment."

Thomas hesitated. "Mama will join us, won't she?"

Nash smiled and glanced down at Laura, who was cuddled up to him still.

"I will be along in a moment, Thomas," she promised. "I just have a few more things to say to your father."

"Good. Don't take too long," Thomas said as he turned away, speaking to Liam as they started back. Nash heard every word. "No, she's too heavy for you to carry, Liam. And Papa said it's my job to look after her until she's bigger."

"I'm big enough to help," Liam argued as the trio reached the doorway, where a maid was waiting.

Nash sighed and looked down at Laura. "So we go back."

"No, Nash. We go forward. Together."

Laura slipped an arm around his back and together they headed slowly toward their children, where they would continue to learn how to be a happy family.

Laura stopped and looked up at him. "I have a confession to make."

"You can tell me anything," he said, turning her to face him.

She wrung her hands. "I lied to you when I came back. When we were talking about Isabelle."

He caught her gaze. "What about Isabelle?"

"It's not really about her." She sighed. "I hadn't really changed my mind about having more children. I was simply afraid that if you knew, you would end up in my bed again. I do still want a dozen."

Nash burst out laughing. He wiped at his eyes, overcome by unexpected emotion. "A dozen? Still? After all we've been through?"

She shrugged. "We're only a quarter of the way through my plan for our family, darling."

"I like the sound of that."

"More children?"

"No. *Darling*. You never called me that before," he said, and kissed her soundly.

Her hands fluttered against his cheek and then cupped his face firmly, ending the kiss. "Darling," she said more loudly, and then kissed him again. When she drew back, she glanced at her bare ring finger. "Tomorrow we're going riding to fetch my wedding ring back."

Nash dug into his pocket and showed her the wreckage of his own. "I need a repair, and a larger one."

She grinned. "When you go to London to help marry off your brother, perhaps?"

"We're going together. All of us," he announced, bending down to whisper against her lips. "I'm not going anywhere without you ever again."

"Papa! Supper is growing cold," Liam bellowed, startling them, and he looked up to find the boy hanging half out of the open window of their apartment sitting room. "I'm so hungry! Mama must be, too."

They both laughed.

"We're coming!" Nash yelled back to his second son, surprised to realize he'd never once yelled at his children for the fun of it before. "They're so impatient."

"Yes, and so will I be for later tonight," Laura confessed. "And you won't ever need that small room you planned to sleep in. You'll be with me tonight and every night to come.

And then hitched up her skirts and ran into the house, giggling.

Nash wasted no time in giving chase.

EPILOGUE

LAURA OPENED her eyes to find Nash at the open window, overlooking the lush gardens of the Ravenswood estate awakening to a new day. He took a sip of his morning tea, closed his eyes, and Laura heard a deep sigh.

It was a perfect day for her too. A new beginning.

And like no day she'd ever experienced...or hadn't in a very long time.

Laura sat up, tucked a few pillows behind her back and made herself comfortable in their new bed.

Nash heard her and rushed to pour a cup of tea to bring to her. She set it aside immediately and pulled him back into bed, determined to be clear about her expectations for him. She kissed him soundly on the lips.

When she freed him, he settled himself at her side and smiled. "Good morning, my love."

"Good morning," she said, dropping another kiss on his cheek. "What are you doing up so early?"

He kissed her back. "I couldn't sleep. I have spent half the night watching you instead."

"And the other half making love to me," she whispered, blushing at the memory of all they had done in the dark.

"Well, you did mention you wouldn't mind another child. It's my duty to pleasure you to make that happen."

"All that is actually required is for you to take your pleasure with *me*," she reminded him.

"Where is the fun in that?" he said, and then he kissed her neck, her shoulder, and his hand rose to cup her breast. Slowly, he lowered her nightgown from her shoulder and continued dropping kisses along her bared skin. "I never wanted our nights to end."

"It's always been so unfair how easily you can excite me," she whispered.

"The feeling has always been mutual. I resented having to leave you."

"Mama?" Liam called suddenly, shocking her with his silent arrival at the door.

"To be continued, my sweet wife," Nash promised as raised her nightgown back into place over her shoulder before he moved away. "Good morning, Liam."

"Thomas is awake, too, and so is Isabelle," Liam confessed, eyes wide. "She was awake before any of us. Will she always do that?"

"Probably." Laura slipped from the bed and threw a robe over her nightgown. "We had best get her."

Laura went to their daughter and changed her, then immediately put her down on the floor to play. The little girl went straight to Thomas and cried with happiness when she reached him. Laura backed toward the door, watching her children with pride.

Nash suddenly pulled her close, his arms enveloping her in a warm embrace. "Come back to bed. We'll leave the door open."

"Are you sure you can restrain yourself?" she teased.

"Of course, I can," he whispered, kissing her forehead, her cheek, her throat. "I know I never said it enough before, but I love you. More than anything or anyone."

Laura looked up at him, filled with happiness from his confession. "I love you too," she whispered, cupping his face. "I'm so grateful that we found our way back to each other."

"You'll never be without me again," Nash promised as he took her hand, leading her back to her bed, where he fussed with her blankets and brought her a fresh cup of tea. He went to stir the fire and toasted bread for each of them, too. She fell even more in love with him when he tried to feed her a bite of toast in bed, and they ended up laughing about it.

Life together was a brand new adventure and Laura couldn't wait to see what happened next.

Algernon Sweet, Duke of Ravenswood, rubbed his hands together gleefully after he scurried away to the main part of the house, where he could not hear his brother's family finally behaving like one.

He was born to be a matchmaker for his brothers. There was nothing more satisfying than knowing those he loved had found their match. He'd helped his cousin Amity reunite with her first love, kept out of Stratford's way while he pursued his choice, and separated Nash from his children on purpose so that Jasper had a chance to prove himself to Sophie.

But he was most proud of his interference in Nash's marriage. Forcing him and Laura under the same roof, making them talk to each other honestly, had given him great satisfaction. He just wished it hadn't taken them almost all of the thirty days to get there.

The women of his family made their men so happy.

Now he was finally free to pursue his own agenda at last. To take a bride who would bear him a son and heir one day soon, he hoped.

His good mood died though.

His bride, his duchess, would not bring him the same joy as his brother's happy marriages did for them. He would not be marrying for love, but for duty. Still, his way was clear at last.

He would arrange his own marriage when he returned to London in the new year and that would be that. The family would be settled and at peace. Such a thing had not been possible until now.

He startled as he heard two thumps on his right and turned quickly. A pair of dark eyes regarded him solemnly out of a wrinkled face. He forced a smile. "Aunt Violet, you're up unexpectedly early today. I trust nothing is wrong?"

"Everything is wrong," she complained, scowling. "We need to talk."

WILD RANDALLS SERIES

Engaging the Enemy ~ Forsaking the Prize

Guarding the Spoils ~ Hunting the Hero

*

SAINTS AND SINNERS SERIES

The Duke and I ~ A Gentleman's Vow

An Earl of Her Own ~ The Lady Tamed

A Necessary Wife

*

REBEL HEARTS SERIES

The Wedding Affair ~ An Affair of Honor

The Christmas Affair ~ An Affair so Right

*

MISS MAYHEM SERIES

Miss Watson's First Scandal

Miss George's Second Chance

Miss Radley's Third Dare

Miss Merton's Last Hope

ABOUT THE AUTHOR

USA Today Bestselling Author Heather Boyd believes every character she creates deserves their own happily-ever-after—no matter how much trouble she puts them through. With that goal in mind, she writes steamy romances that skirt the boundaries of propriety to keep readers enthralled until the wee hours of the morning. Heather has published over sixty regency romance novels and shorter works full of daring seductions and distinguished rogues. She lives north of Sydney, Australia, with her trio of rogues and a fluffy four-legged overlord.

Learn more about Heather at:
www.Heather-Boyd.com